Unsuitable Celibate?

Mistaken Glory of Celibacy!

Bharat S. Thakkar, Ph.D.

Printed in the United States of America

| ISBN: | Softcover | 979-8-88622-656-0 |
| | eBook | 979-8-88622-657-7 |

Republished by: PageTurner Press and Media LLC
Publication Date: 09/28/2022

To order copies of this book, contact:
PageTurner Press and Media
Phone: 1-888-447-9651
info@pageturner.us
www.pageturner.us

Unsuitable Celibate?

Mistaken Glory of Celibacy!

Bharat S. Thakkar, Ph.D.

To

Jitendra 'Jitu' Patel, my childhood friend from Vadodara, India, and now in Atlanta, Georgia. Our friendship has only strengthened with the passage of time and I cherish that.

Dr. Bharat Thakkar

Jitendra 'Jitu' Patel

Bharat and I have been friends since the 5th grade. This friendship of sixty plus years, in India and in America, is full of fond memories. As teenagers, we both had similar interests and hobbies. Whether it was studying for the 1st rank in the class or playing Ping-Pong hours at a time, we competed. But Bharat would always come out a step ahead of me. Once again, in dedicating this book to me, Bharat, you prove that you are way ahead of me. Here you honor our friendship by dedication of this book, and I have nothing in return to match it! All I can say is thank you, pal. Your literary creations have never ceased to amaze me.

Jitendra Patel, Duluth (Atlanta), GA, USA

The story of 'Unsuitable Celibate' has played out in mind for at least two decades. It has been plotted and plotted again over the years. Although the basic plot has remained pretty much the same, details have changed. It is a world I understand rather well because it is a world I have experienced up close.

I was mindful while forming the narrative that I avoid offending anyone for the sake of offending. On the other hand, if people choose to take offense because that is an easy thing to do these days, then I suppose there is nothing I can do.

'Unsuitable Celibate' at its heart is about choice. We all have a natural right to choose but oftentimes that natural right is diluted by the vagaries of life.

Having lived in America for close to 50 years, I am very much a part of the evolution of the Indian American community over a considerable period. Those decades have given me a good sense of a community living conflicted between two cultures, one they bring with them and the other they adopt here. However, there is a third crucial element to this and that is of the generations born here. They may have been born into culturally rooted Indian families but on their own, they are very much like mainstream Americans. Their conflicts and dilemmas are of a completely different nature.

My short novel is an exploration into these sociocultural pulls and pressures without being judgmental about them.

The novella is written as if its fictional protagonist Parthiv Patel was commissioned by a fictional publishing house called Prem Publishing. And I am merely bringing it to your attention.

Bharat S, Thakkar, Ph.D.
Wheaton, Illinois.

'Unsuitable Celibate' by Parthiv Patel A Brief Note:

I had to write my story. The only question was whether I should do it in first-person or third- person. I would have liked it in first-person because it feels as if I am owning it up unlike in third- person which seems like I am keeping a safe distance from it. In the end, the word of my editor at Prem Publishing prevailed and I agreed to do it in third-person. So here it is. It is my story but told as if it is someone else's. None of that changes its elements.

--Parthiv Patel

CONTENTS

PROLOGUE

As a 14-year-old in 1979, Ramnik Patel came precariously close to becoming a monk and being forced to lead a life of celibacy. His parents Tribhuvan and Chandrika were diehard followers of a Hindu sect that demanded that at least one male member of the devotee families was committed to the religious order. Had it not been for his tuberculosis his parents, who lived on the outskirts of Ahmedabad, would have happily given him away to the religious order.

Although as a teenager he was happy that he dodged the bullet, in his adult years he had frequently wondered with a tinge of regret what could have been. When he saw ordinary devotees fall at the feet of the monks, he felt an overpowering sense of loss. He was not so sure how he would have coped with lifelong celibacy but believed that there were other spiritual compensations as well as societal rewards, which would have helped him overcome that loss.

He immigrated to America in 1995 on a family green card as a 31-year-old marginally surviving trader in Ahmedabad along with his wife 30-year-old wife Dipti. They decided to live in the Bay Area in California because a large number of their family members and friends lived there. In the first couple of years, they both worked at various motels before managing to raise enough money to invest in a grocery store on East El Camino Real, Sunnyvale. Without the slightest effort to be creative, they called the store Patel-India Groceries, drawing on the obvious name recognition of both Patel and India.

Their son Parthiv was born in 1998. On the day he was born, they decided not to have any more children even though they knew that there was a very real possibility that the sect that they followed could well claim him. While the Patels seemed to be reasonably flexible in their everyday life and in raising Parthiv, there were lines they would never cross. They made sure Parthiv learned that. Although there was some recognizable evolution in the way both Ramnik and Dipti viewed the sect, including on the question of pledging their son to it, they very much remained wedded to its cause.

In 2014, when Parthiv turned 16 and graduated, the Patels confronted the eventuality, which Ramnik had managed to avoid because of his TB. Parthiv was a perfectly healthy teenager.

CHAPTER 1

On the first day at Sunnyvale High School (SHC), James the jock looked at Parthiv Patel and winced.

"Man! You *are* ugly," he said. For good measure, he had renamed Parthiv Patel Port-a-Potty or Pee Pee.

It was not the first time that Parthiv had heard a version of that comment but it was by far the most direct and unambiguous. Not knowing what to do, he merely ducked as if James's words were a club that had swung too close to his head.

"What cologne are you wearing today, Pee Pee, chicken tikka masala?" James said as his fellow jocks laughed.

Parthiv looked for a rupture in the ground where he could slide in and disappear from the daily torture. Although born in Sunnyvale, Parthiv never really felt welcomed to his city's mainstream from the kindergarten. Once, as he approached his locker he had to walk past the same bunch of football players, one of whom said, "Hey Saddam, have you beheaded anyone lately?" Saddam being Saddam Hussein of Iraq who had only recently been overthrown by President George W. Bush's war.

Parthiv always chose not to say a word in response when he faced continuous ragging. He knew he could not take on any one of the jocks even in his wildest dream.

To compound his plight, his mother would pack the traditional Gujarati lunch for him every day, including the mango pickle, the pungently smelling methiya keri. James the jock once caught a whiff from Parthiv's lunchbox. "Damn! Did you steal that from Saddam's weapons of mass destruction? I think President Bush should invade your home next," James had said once much to the amusement of a passing teacher who realized his transgression and quickly apologized to Parthiv and upbraided James. Even Parthiv could not help laughing at this offensive crack at his expense. He noticed a perceptible softening in James' attitude after that. It was as if by making Parthiv complicit in his racist humor, he had partially accepted him.

Growing up for Parthiv was an archetypal experience of a classic victim of bullying. Most of the taunts and barbs were predictable and yet hurtful. He internalized them so much that every time he heard one he would reflexively gulp.

If he did not feel accepted at school, he also did not feel at home at home either. His parents Ramnik and Dipti never seemed to have emerged from their own formative years in the India generally and Ahmedabad particularly of the 1960s and 70s. Ramnik still got his clothes tailored by Shivabhai Tailors, Ratan Pol, Ahmedabad. He wore pleated trousers and poplin shirts made from "cut-pieces" sold by weight right outside Shivabhai Tailors. Dipti, comparatively more assimilated in American life, bought her pants and tops from Wal-Mart. Their presence at PTA meetings was long a source of quiet embarrassment for Parthiv because it served no purpose other than reinforcing the stereotype about him among his fellow students.

Although there were many greatly redeeming moments during his four years in high school—like the first time he met classmate and now best friend George O'Keefe—what remained a predominant memory were insults and humiliation by James and his kind. It was only during the last six months of his final year that he had managed to develop thick skin and even some pushback. That still did not stop snide attacks and derision. "Which harbor did your parents get off at?" That was one of the questions asked of him even on the evening of his school graduation. It was, of course, a reference to the term FOB or fresh off the boat. "The SOB is FOB", was one of the more vicious comments passed against Parthiv.

Now that he was emerging from that tunnel and preparing for his graduation, he was unsure about how he felt. Over the past four years, he had become strangely comfortable with his life at school. At least the bullies there had familiar faces. Whenever he saw certain boys approaching, he could predict the ordeal that would follow. Somehow, that familiarity and predictability mitigated some of the pain and anguish he felt on a daily basis.

In contrast, he realized he did not know what to expect when he would join university. He had almost decided not to go to university and instead join his father's modest grocery business on El Camino Real. He was not particularly drawn to the business but he knew he would not have to struggle to find a slot for himself in a familiar environment. He was not answerable to anyone other than his father who, in any case, was keen to have him take over the business and expand it.

In one of his diary entries, Parthiv had written, "The smell of hing is weirdly comforting. It is an awful smell but it is familiar, kind of like all the torture the jocks subjected me to." Much of his packed lunch's smell came from either a combination of garlic/onion or hing or ajwain (carom seeds) or all of them together. It was only towards the end of his high school that Parthiv had gathered enough courage to counter taunts and insults about his food. He would explain hing by its English name asafetida, also known as 'Devil's dung', making it only worse because some of them retorted saying "You mean a fetid ass?" He would try to mislead his classmates by saying that asafetida had strong aphrodisiac qualities which explained why Indians were so virile. He once told James the jock that hing led to an hours-long erection. James shot back saying, "I will need that when I am in my 80s."

In the days leading up to the graduation ceremony, Parthiv had become the most comfortable he had ever been with school and his mates. In fact, he had even begun to discover some redeeming traits even in his professed nemesis James the jock. He had told his mother with a trace of gratitude and relief that despite all his ill will James had never been physical with him. "Not once did he touch me or push me around," Parthiv had said reminiscing about high school two days before graduation.

The graduation ceremony was a tame affair for Parthiv. A solid straight B- and C+ student, he had no expectations to be conferred any honors or awards that day. He wore his graduation cap and gown with as much reluctance and disregard as he could muster unlike those straight 'A' students who had taken tutorials about the etiquettes of wearing the two. The cap had to be worn one inch above the eyebrow and the tassel had to be on the right side of their face as per the requirements of the Sunnyvale High School. He just slapped the cap on at a random angle with the tassel facing the back and the gown not fully buttoned.

Most parents cheered aloud when their son or daughter's names were called. Parthiv's parents sat looking anxious. His mother applauded as an afterthought. Parthiv carried his graduation certificate as if it was toxic and started removing the gown almost as soon as he got off the stage.

In a rare show of paternal emotion, Ramnik ruffled his son's hair and said, "Dikra (son), life's responsibilities will start soon." Dipti gave him a long hug.

Just as he was getting into his parents car, James had grabbed his shoulder from behind and shook his hand, saying, "No hard feelings Pee Pee. It's all cool, dude." James then walked off with a couple of girls.

Returning home in their Toyota Corolla, Ramnik and Dipti sounded happy but could not shake off a phone call they had received that morning and whose content they had not yet revealed to their son. It was from the Siddhi Prapti Sansthan (The Institute for the Attainment of Siddhi), a sect whose founder and precepts they followed with unquestioned devotion. The caller was polite but firmly insistent that they bring Parthiv to the institute's sprawling campus at Bear Valley Trail in Napa, California at the earliest.

That evening the Patels had organized a big dinner to celebrate his graduation. The extended Patel clan had been invited as had Bela Amin, his childhood sweetheart and her family, father Mahendra and mother Meena. Bela was a year junior to Parthiv at SHC. She looked older than her 15 years. Her physical attributes were not lost on anyone. In fact, more often than Parthiv's close friendship with Bela earned him the grudging respect of the jocks at school who thought if a girl as good looking as her found him worthwhile, he had to have something special in him.

Although Ramnik and Dipti were expecting the call from the Sansthan, they were hoping it would come much after Parthiv had graduated from university and certainly not on the very day of his high school graduation. It was the kind of call that most Sansthan followers both dreaded and yet eventually complied with.

The call was always full of verve and reassurance. The caller, usually a member of an elite group of 10 swamis tasked with the job after a rigorous training, always sounded sanguine and upbeat. Such callers spoke precise language that was carefully crafted so as not to sound predatory but in fact as a harbinger of divine blessing that was reserved for the chosen few. The callers were trained with a specifically designed manual, which only those tasked with the job of making such calls and the Sansthan chief had access to.

The Patels had followed the Sansthan for the better part of their lives and felt beholden to it in ways that were hard for others in the Indian American community to understand. A summons, a call, or an invitation from the Sansthan took precedence over everything in life among the followers who were mostly hardworking and decent people. The personal life may not be as dead as it was in Russia after the 1917 revolution but it always came a poor second to the demands of the Sansthan. The Sansthan was a beguiling presence in the followers' lives even though it did a lot of public good. However, the public good was encouraged as long as it also unambiguously advanced the Sansthan's cause.

Parthiv grew up in the shadow of the Sansthan without quite realizing how dominant its influence had been until the time he was about to find out that evening. The Patels did not want to tell him about the call as long as they could fob off their visible nervousness and anxiety with an alibi. When Ramnik told Parthiv "Dikra (son), life's responsibilities will start soon" he was making a direct reference to the call without really letting his son in on that.

The Sansthan was so omnipresent in the Patel household that right from his infancy Parthiv had seen only its exhortations, aphorisms and wisdoms displayed on various walls. There was only one portrait that was displayed in their home, that of someone Parthiv knew only as "Guruji." It was portrait of a man at once severe and hypnotic in his gaze. The black and white portrait, which was found in all homes of the Sansthan followers, showed

Guruji looking unwaveringly into the camera which turned out to be of an American photographer named Kevin Church, who went on to become his devotee and stayed in India until his death at the age 67 in 1981. The Patels wanted Guruji's portrait even in Parthiv's room but he had resisted it.

One of the exhortations that were drilled into Parthiv's mind from his childhood was, "Life is sacrifice. Sacrifice is life." For a child those were nothing more than incomprehensible words put together. It was only now that he was a ripe teenager that he had begun to get some measure of what they meant. Why life had to be sacrifice was something totally lost on him.

Parthiv had also begun to notice some of the books published by the Sansthan that his father read. One of them was titled 'Celibacy and Restraint: Ingredients of a Happy Life". It was written by Guruji in the 1960s and had been updated somewhat to meet the changing idiom among the new generations of followers. The basic message, however, remained the same as captured in the very first lines of the first chapter. They read, "It falls only on the chosen ones to lead a life of celibacy and restraint. It is a tough path to follow but eventually the only worthwhile path to follow…."

It was not as if Parthiv had been told these things explicitly because he was still too young. But in the last year or so Ramnik had started to subtly talk about what sex meant and why it should be avoided as much as one could. Ramnik was awkward talking about the subject of sex. Six months earlier, when Parth had turned 16, he had sat his son down and struggled to explain. He had only botched it. "Beta, you are at an age when doing sex and touching girls would be natural," he said as Parthiv burst out laughing. "Dad, what do you mean, "doing sex and touching girls"? We have been taught everything at school. You don't have to teach me."

Simultaneously relieved that his son already knew and slighted that he was not the one to explain it first, Ramnik had said trying to establish his paternal authority, "You are not going to do sex before you have talked to your mother and me." Parthiv had chosen not to reply.

On the evening of the graduation, the mood was somewhat somber for the Patels. Parthiv went to his room before the party as his parents stood around the kitchen island staring at each other not saying a word but understanding each that was left unsaid. Finally, Dipti broke the nervous silence.

"When should we tell him? I think we should not. The Sansthan will eventually give up," she said.

Ramnik, scratching an imaginary itch on his chin, replied, "I don't think we can keep it from him for longer than a few days. The Sansthan will call again very soon. In fact, Dhirubhai (the caller) said as much. He said Swamiji wanted to know as soon as this weekend."

"He is our son and not the Swamiji's or the Sansthan's son. We will do what is best for him and we will do it when it best for him," Dipti said with a firmness that surprised Ramnik.

"But Dipti you know how it is. We have to live with the same people. We cannot keep stalling them without losing our relationships," Ramnik said. "Many of them are coming tonight and they will ask."

"If they ask, ask them to talk to me. I know what to tell them," Dipti said.

"What will you tell them? What can you possibly tell them?" Ramnik persisted.

"I will tell them that tonight is Parthiv's night and everything else is secondary," she said.

"I forgot to tell you that Dhuribhai also said Swamiji would call to personally congratulate Parthiv on his graduation. I hope that he does not directly ask Parthiv," Ramnik said.

"I will talk to Swamiji before he speaks with Parthiv. I will tell him that we will break the news to him at our pace and the time of our choosing," she said.

The phone rang then startling both Ramnik and Dipti. It was Dhirubhai again. "Yes, Dhirubhai," Dipti said.

"I am calling to find out when it would be the best time for Swamiji to speak to Parthiv. As you know Swamiji retires by 8.30," Dhirubhai said.

Dipti saw an opening in that and seized it. "Why don't we keep the call for the weekend during the day? You know how teenagers are. Parthiv may want to be with his friends tonight. I suggest we do it over the weekend," she said.

There was a brief silence at the other end and then came the reply, "That is fine too. I will let Swamiji know. But remember what Ramnikbhai and I spoke about earlier. Parthiv has a great opportunity to serve the Sansthan. Swamiji is very excited for him."

The Swamiji whose presence loomed over that happy family evening was Swami Raghu Vishwa.

CHAPTER 2

Swami Raghu Vishwa had one favorite pastime when he went perambulating around the inner compound of the Sansthan campus. He liked to caress the flowers and leaves of wild anise that were abundant in his ashram at Bear Valley Trail in Napa, California. He told his followers that the touch of wild anise reminded him of "the glory of sentience."

Vishwa was a slight but sharply defined figure who had mastered the art of beatific smile. At 76, he did not look much older than 50. However, at 50, he looked his age as the only photograph of his in his sparse office showed. He seemed to smile and laugh a lot. In the photograph, he smiled so wide that it appeared to spill out of the frame.

He came to America when he was 24 to expand the base of the institute, which was until then mainly limited to a few ashrams in Haridwar and surrounding pre-Himalayan hills. Swami Sadhu Vishwa, the founder of the order, was already 86 when he found Vishwa as an 18-year-old roaming along the ghat of Har ki Pauri in 1956. Sadhu Vishwa saw in the joyful teenager a spirit that he said was like the rushing waters of the Ganga.

In 1962, at age 92, as he prepared to take Samadhi he told Raghu Vishwa, "The Sansthan needs to spread its message outside India. America is where you are needed. For India, my legacy alone is enough."

Raghu Vishwa left for America a week after Sadhu Vishwa had "elevated himself to the ultimate destination of consciousness". In simpler terms, Sadhu Vishwa had essentially starved himself to death. The running of the main ashram in Haridwar was entrusted to Swami Tapeshwar Vishwa with the clear instruction from Sadhu Vishwa that Raghu was his successor.

The ashram in Bear Valley Trail was a monument to the Sansthan's extraordinary ability to marshal resources that they did not own and generate funds that did not really exist to build a highly impressive establishment. The main temple's curvilinear shikhara or tower rose to 300 feet with four subsidiary towers, each rising 150 feet. The pinkish yellow stone was shipped from India fully carved and sculpted to precise dimensions laid down by the Sansthan's in-house architects and sculptors. It took Raghu Vishwa over two years to complete the shipping before he could give the go ahead for its assembly at Bear Valley.

The garbhagriha, literally the womb-room, or sanctum sanctorum and the main prayer hall together were 10,000 square feet covered with pink and white Makrana marble. The pantheon in the garbhagriha was the traditional Hindu combination of Shiv, Vishnu, Krishna, Amba, Ganesh and Hanuman but the Sansthan had ensured that the presence of its founder Swami Sadhu Vishwa was not lost on anyone. There was a marble statue of his sitting in the lotus position in an alcove lighted in pinkish-orange recessed lighting from the top and two sides. The statue's inspiration was a 1948 photograph of Sadhu Vishwa taken by Kevin Church. It was a more personable photograph than the one hanging in Sansthan households.

The statue froze in marble a youthful Sadhu Vishwa. While no specific attempts were made by any of his main successors to perpetuate the myth of Sadhu Vishwa's eternal youth, the Sansthan staff did not correct devotees either when they concluded that the statue captured him when he was 90. They figured that all subtle mythmaking could only help further the mystique of the man and the Sansthan. It, in fact, was a carefully planned as well as serendipitously discovered accumulation of myths about Sadhu Vishwa and, to a lesser degree, about Raghu Vishwa.

Raghu Vishwa recognized early on that being in America and dealing with Indians of a very different class compared to the Sansthan's core base in India, he had to evolve a new style of attracting followers and funds. Unlike the founder, who retained a lot of the old-school asceticism and austere lifestyle of wandering mendicants, Raghu Vishwa knew he had to introduce an element of "subtle spiritual ostentation" to the Sansthan operations in America. He also had to keep in mind the generations of Indians being born in America with next to no awareness about their cultural and religious roots.

In the early 1960s when he first began the Sansthan first began to strike roots, Raghu Vishwa still enjoyed the advantage of having to deal with a majority of Indians who were still very much culturally rooted in India and things Indian. Being new immigrants they steadfastly maintained a separate identity, most of which came from a combination of cultural traditions and religious practices and rituals. That he arrived in an America mesmerized by the Beatles barely six months after they burst open over the country's cultural landscape in November, 1963, may be entirely coincidental. However, the force with which they had captivated the popular imagination had served to soften up the average American mind to external influences. Although the Beatles' association with India, Maharishi Mahesh Yogi and Transcendental Meditation (TM) was still four years into the future, he had already become well known in America after he first came in 1959. He extensively taught TM in Los Angeles, San Francisco, Boston and New York.

Sitting 10,000 miles away in India, Sadhu Vishwa had been keeping abreast of Mahesh Yogi's sojourns and made up his mind to carve out a little piece of this spiritual real estate for his Sansthan as well. The chronology of his spotting Raghu Vishwa in 1956, Mahesh Yogi in America three years later, the Beatles' visit in 1963 and his disciple's eventual arrival in April, 1964 may have happened fortuitously but the way Sansthan went about mining a growing fascination for things Indian was rather systematic. Throughout the decades of the 1960s-1980s Raghu Vishwa traveled across America offering a series of lectures and yoga lessons even while incorporating the Sansthan's core philosophy that encouraged at least one male member of Hindu families joining the order. He understood that it was potentially controversial and hence in the early years pitched it in a manner that appealed to the audience.

His typical pitch went like this: "Spirituality is as much an individual pursuit as it is a collective calling. If we as a society want to attain a degree of spiritual centeredness, it is essential that institutions such as the Sansthan not only survive but get infused with new blood on a regular basis. An institution like ours is as good as new and young as people who join it with a sense of lifelong commitment to its objectives. I appeal to you to consider taking part in this grand mission together for it is not the Sansthan's mission but humanity's mission."

On the face of it, it was hard to find fault with this mission statement. It was both ambitious and voluntary. To most outsiders who came in contact with the Sansthan and its various activities on a perfunctory basis, everything appeared to be unexceptionable. The physical infrastructure of the ashram played a big part in conveying this image. In fact, Raghu Vishwa even believed that the flora of the campus also played a crucial role in creating an overall sense of non-judgmental serenity. However, beneath that blissful calm rumbled an agenda that was not entirely inspiring. It was essentially a business enterprise that employed all the marketing techniques, including training their recruits, to sell a product that was supposed to be ephemeral—spirituality. From the dress code to the hierarchy, everything was meticulously planned.

The top tier of the religious order wore an ochre dhoti and a loose buttoned up, collarless shirt with a deeper red intricately woven piping around the sleeve-ends. The rest of the monks wore plain rust yellowish dhoti and V-neck shirt. Raghu Vishwa and Tapeshwar Vishwa wore a somewhat elongated brimless hat that created the illusion of making them appear taller than they were. Guruji's attire of white dhoti with a black lining and a black angvastram was retired after his death like the retiring the number of an athlete.

During major events, when the ashram put up a big portrait of Guruji in the midst of the prayer hall, it made a striking contrast against a sea of rust yellow in the middle represented by ordinary monks and the ochre edge represented by the upper echelon. Like all religions, the visual coordination of the Sansthan clergy was carefully designed.

The kind of call that the Patels received on the day of Parthiv's graduation was all too common and, more often than not, successful in that it coerced impressionable and unwilling young men into joining the order. The role of the parents in this endeavor was rather dubious because it was they who invariably colluded with the Sansthan to push young men, mostly in their mid-teens, into of what one man who left the order described as a "life of spiritual servitude". The man, 28-year-old Paresh Mehta of Jersey City, spent close to 13 years in the Sansthan after his widow mother was talked into committing him to it against his wishes. It reached a stage for Paresh where he would openly fight with the order about its "hidden agenda". When he left the Sansthan in 2010, Sansthan was more relieved than Paresh because his presence and constant complaining meant terrible PR.

In an interview with *The Edison Examiner* that year, he accused the Sansthan of "egregious deception" in their campaign to recruit "gullible young Indian American teenagers and confine them to a life of bogus spiritual bliss". It was in that interview that he had described the Sansthan as a "life of spiritual servitude". Stung by the criticism, the Sansthan did something unprecedented. Raghu Vishwa issued a personally signed statement "comprehensively rejecting" all claims made by Paresh.

The statement said: "The Sansthan is a spiritual order that has been in existence since 1895 and in its long history distinguished itself as a passionate advocate of Bharatvarsh's millennia old culture, traditions and wisdom. It goes against the very fundamentals of our philosophy to compel anyone to join the order against their wish. We strongly refute and denounce reckless and malicious assertions made by one of our former and deeply disgruntled members. It is not our tradition to engage in legal battles because we are fully reassured about our moral and spiritual strengths. The publication of the interview by *The Edison Examiner* is aimed at gratuitously damaging our reputation. We are happy to point out that the Sansthan's credibility and standing are far bigger than an individual's malicious vendetta. May Paresh Mehta find his own bliss."

The smugly self-assured tone of the statement, which was written by Raghu Vishwa, had the desired effect. It discredited Paresh and, in a weird way, bolstered the Sansthan's standing among the community. Since the Paresh Mehta affair, during the passage of four years, the Sansthan stepped up its efforts to recruit novice monks. According to informal estimates discussed among the families of the followers, in the four years since the Paresh Mehta case almost upended it, the Sansthan had managed to bring in 75 teenagers, the oldest among those were 20-years-old by 2014. At 16, Parthiv was the right age.

Raghu Vishwa returned from his stroll on the evening of Parthiv's graduation and summoned Dhirubhai.

"Did you talk to Ramnikbhai?" he asked even as peeled an orange grown on the Sansthan's farmland. Before eating the orange, he squeezed its rind in his hands and rubbed them. He then sectioned it and meticulously removed the pith before eating small pieces.

"I spoke to Diptiben. She suggested that you speak to Parthiv over the weekend," Dhirubhai said, conscious that Raghu Vishwa did not like to wait when it came to new recruits.

"Why wait? Let us call now. It is 8.15 and the party would have started. Parthiv should be home," Raghu Vishwa said with a firmness that Dhuribhai knew after having spent decades with him meant some annoyance at having been asked to wait.

Dhirubhai, who had family relations with the Patels because his niece was married to Ramnik's older brother Mukesh's son Rakesh, was hesitant but helpless. He waited for a few seconds to see if Raghu Vishwa would change his mind. He did not and looked at him disapprovingly. Dhirubhai redialed the Patels.

CHAPTER 3

All guests had arrived at the three-bedroom Patel condominium bearing mostly envelopes containing checks and cash. The preferred denomination was $101 with those from the immediate family carrying $501. By a rough estimate, the evening's tally would easily touch $10,000, which was supposed to go towards Parthiv's school fee.

Bela came with $1001 and an urgent urge to kiss Parthiv. Dressed in a yellow sunflower bomber jacket and strapless black Palazzo Pants Jumpsuit the five feet six inches Bela looked stunning. When she arrived Parthiv whistled and said, "Are you sure you got the right house? I am not expecting someone so hot." Finding no one was looking, Bela quickly kissed him standing in the vestibule. It was their first kiss since the two had made a pact to do it on his graduation. Just as they pulled away from each other, the landline phone rang.

Dipti saw the caller ID that said Sansthan and ignored it. Five minutes later, it rang again. This time, Ramnik saw it and answered. It was Dhirubhai.

"Swamiji wants to congratulate Parthiv. We called earlier but no one answered," Dhirubhai said. As if right on cue, Raghu Vishwa put on his beatific smile even though Ramnik could not see him.

"Ramnikbhai, Kem chho? Havey to dikro moto thava mandyo. (How are you? Son has started to grow up now)," Raghu Vishwa said.

Under ordinary circumstances, that last observation would not have meant anything other than what it conveyed but coming from Raghu Vishwa it was loaded with meaning which Ramnik did not like.

"Yes, yes. Time moves fast. It seems like yesterday that I took him to kindergarten," Ramnik said.

"It couldn't be yesterday," Raghu Vishwa joked and both laughed. "May I give Parthiv my blessings now?"

Ramnik went looking for Parthiv as he ran into Dipti who asked, "Who is calling?" Ramnik covered the mouthpiece and made a whispering sound to say, "Swamiji". Dipti looked angry and troubled. "Why did you answer?" she said in whispers. Parthiv happened to come to them with Bela and said, "Dad, mom, Bela is looking stunning tonight." Ramnik and Dipti hugged Bela.

Ramnik took Parthiv aside and handed him the phone, "Le vaat kar Swamiji sathey. (Here talk to Swamiji)."

Caught unawares by it he said out aloud, "Not now dad!" Raghu Vishwa heard that.

Parthiv came on the line and said, "Hello Swamiji."

"Son, I heard you but I understand. I just wanted to congratulate you. My congratulations on your graduation. There is a whole life ahead of you now. Don't forget the Sansthan is paying attention. Let's meet soon," he said.

"Sure Swamiji. Thank you and I am sorry about earlier," Parthiv said. The call ended as Ramnik and Parthiv looked at each other, unsure about what to say.

Bela came and broke the tension saying, "Thiv, let's have fun with the cousins."

Parthiv had ten cousins, four boys and six girls. Except one family, none of the others followed the Sansthan. The one family that followed the Sansthan was that of his schoolmate Jayendra 'Jay' Kothari. Parthiv did not know if his family too had received the phone call. Just as he was about to ask Jay his father Jasubhai approached with his mobile.

"Say Pranam to Swamiji," he said handing him the phone.

Jay rolled his eyes and answered, "Pranam, Swamiji. Yes, thank you so much…Yes, I am very happy…Yes sir, I will do that."

He returned the mobile to his father and said, "Dad, did you have to do it now? I don't like that man at all."

Jasubhai was taken aback by his son's rather candid comment. "You cannot talk about Swamiji like that. He is our guru. Ek lafo marish. (I will slap you)." Realizing he was in the midst of others, he walked off in a huff.

Jay asked Parthiv, "Did that jerk call you too?" Parthiv, "He did."

"Did he say 'Don't forget the Sansthan is paying attention'?" Jay asked.

"He did," replied Parthiv.

"What an asshole," Jay said. The cousins laughed.

In the large family room, Ramnik and Jasubhai were engaged in an animated conversation.

"Jayendra needs severe disciplining. The ashram will do him good. He uses such offensive language about Swamiji," Jasubhai said.

"That's not right but Swamiji should have waited for a few days before calling. They are just 16 and they have just graduated. What do they care about life?" Ramnik said.

"I have made up my mind. Jayendra will join next month," Jasubhai said.

"Isn't that too soon? You are creating a rebel. Give him some time. Let him enjoy his break. Do you even know what happens at the ashram? I hear terrible stories," Ramnik said.

"Listen, you keep your bogus fears to yourself. The Sansthan needs young men to continue its mission. We have to sacrifice for them," Jasubhai said.

"Yes but give the boy some time," Ramnik said.

Watching the two men from the corner of their eyes, Dipti and Jyoti, the two respective wives knew something heated was afoot. They both walked up to their husbands and asked, "Are you two arguing again?"

Ramnik laughed half a laugh and said, "Oh no we are just talking about the boys and their future."

Jyoti, perhaps the strongest objector of the Sansthan among the four, said to Jasu, "You will send Jayendra to the Sansthan over my dead body."

"It is up to you if you want to die so soon," Jasubhai said and realized that he had crossed the line trying to be funny. The other three were shell-shocked by what they heard.

"Jasubhai, what are you saying? Do you really mean that?" asked Dipti, her voice loud enough for others to hear.

The joyous hubbub that pervaded the room halted temporarily as the guests strained to find out what was going on. The four broke up and went their own way. Ramnik went to one group of guests and said, "Oh that was nothing. We were arguing about India's elections and Jasubhai said something about Rahul Gandhi. Dipti was surprised to hear that. She knows we all support Narendrabhai but we can't lose our decorum about others."

Some of the guests sensed that the debate was clearly not about India's politics and something deeper was happening.

That is when Ela Sheth, Ramnik's 32-year-old first cousin, said, "Have you yet received the call?" Everybody understood what the call meant.

Ramnik hesitated before answering. "Swamiji called just to congratulate Parthiv. Dipti has made it clear we will decide what best for him. The Sansthan cannot make that decision," he said.

"I am glad you say that because the others do not even say that. I am sure Jasubhai cannot wait to pack Jay off to Bear Valley. What a loser?" Ela, the chief technology officer of a Silicon Valley startup involved in pioneering data compression algorithm, was perhaps the most outspoken guest that evening. Her reputation as an atheist who could not stand religious intrusions into personal life was well known. She had once got into a rough argument with Raghu Vishwa at a private fundraiser hosted by her company's CEO and co-founder Jignesh Vakharia.

Much to Vakharia's chagrin, Ela had described Raghu Vishwa as a "masquerader" who hid an insidious agenda of "real estate and money-grabbing" behind spirituality. Raghu Vishwa was so shaken by the verbal onslaught that he left the party before the dinner was served. Jignesh and Ela had to spend next one week to sort out their tensions. Jignesh could not fire Ela because she was an equal partner in the startup as well as its key technological brain. She held half a dozen patents in data compression, which were the IP mainstay of the company in which venture capitalists had put their faith. In fact, if there was a weak link in the company it was Jignesh and he knew it well.

Ela enjoyed quite a following among the community's teenage crowd because of her contrarian views, enormous professional success—she had sold her last venture for $75 million—and the fact that she spoke the idiom that they understood. In contrast, Jasubhai and of his ilk were very much frozen in an archaic period that existed mainly in their minds. While Ramnik and Dipti were not so hardcore despite generally erring on the side of the Sansthan, Jyoti was an ardent supporter of Ela.

Had it not been for Dharmesh Daftari, a CPA and much beloved court jester at such gatherings, intervening to end dicey situations, this party too could have been ruined by the tensions caused directly by the dreaded phone call. Dharmesh's signature move was to announce dinner set to the most popular teenage song of the day. He could not sing to save his life but his spirit was so infectious that even the generally disdainful teenage crowd did not mind him. This time he announced that dinner was served in the tune of Jacob Latimore's 'Like em all'. He made it 'Eat em all.'"

Once the food was served, tensions between Jasubhai and Ramnik melted away, and much bonhomie ensued. The immediate order of business was to open the envelopes and count the loot. Being the only CPA in the gathering, the task fell on Dharmesh. He quickly added up 23 checks and 25 cash contributions. The total came to $10,750 or, as he said with characteristic cuteness, "223.958" per person. He then declared, "Although I did give my check, I am going to add an extra

$251 to make it $11001." His objective being to satisfy the belief about not gifting amounts that end in a zero. There is always one extra buck added as if to ensure that the fortune does not fall through the hole or zero at the end.

After dinner and money counting, a local DJ was pressed into service to play hit singles starting with 'Love Never Felt So Good', the Justin Timberlake version Michael Jackson's song. It was chosen by Dharmesh, who was the first to hit the dance floor. He quickly vacated in deference to the teenage crowd.

As the youngsters danced, Ramnik, Dipti, Jasu and Jyoti chatted about everything other than the Sansthan. However, each knew that the other had Raghu Vishwa on their mind.

In his sparse but comfortable bedroom in his ashram, Raghu Vishwa had only sleep on his mind. However, before retiring he told Dhirubhai, "Guruji (Sadhu Vishwa) took his Samadhi in 1962. In 2017, we will mark his 55th death anniversary. Can we initiate 55 new monks by then? Let us make it happen."

CHAPTER 4

Parthiv could not sleep that night. The joy of having graduated had diminished quickly because of the phone call.

Although there was nothing particularly aggressive about Raghu Vishwa's tone, the way he said, "Don't forget the Sansthan is paying attention", worried him. For a 16-year-old, it was a strange thing to be told by someone 60 years his senior.

Parthiv had in the past couple of years become aware of the domineering presence of the Sansthan not just in his household but many other families. He did not pay much attention to it because he had his own problems at school to deal with, courtesy of James. Occasionally, he would hear his father and mother discuss the Sansthan's activities, which were mostly from the standpoint of his own future involvement. He never fully understood what it meant because his parents generally talked in Gujarati. However, the brief conversation with Raghu Vishwa had made it all too real.

A word that he heard often was "Bhramcharya" which he had just discovered meant celibacy. While he may not understand all the implications of celibacy and the life of a renunciate, he was now old enough to understand that it meant no sex. Ever. Jayendra, the go-to guy for all such burning questions that trouble teenagers, had described celibacy thus: "You can take out your dick only to urinate."

Jay's derisive rejection of his father's ideas had concentrated Parthiv's mind in the last couple of hours about what it could possibly mean to him.

Jay sounded like he knew more than Parthiv about the Sansthan and what it represented. The force with which Jay had challenged Jasubhai meant that he had been paying greater attention to it. He knew that unlike his father, Jasubhai had been vocal about preparing Jay for a monk's life. As if to revolt against that, Jay had started smoking by stealing cigarettes from Jasu's packs.

Parthiv finally got out of his bed around 11.30 and went down for breakfast. His parents were already in the kitchen. Dipti was frying some snacks and Ramnik was mumbling shlokas from a tiny booklet. His index finger moved from one line to the next so rapidly Parthiv thought he was in a hurry to finish the ritual. He was. It was a sight he had seen for years but it never failed to amuse him. He finally asked Ramnik what he always wanted to ask.

"Dad, are you even reading it or only showing that you are reading it?"

Ramnik's first impulse was to scold Parthiv for making light of his steadfast commitment but checked himself and smiled. "I have read this since I was your age. I can recite it in the middle of the night," he said.

"Then why do you need the book? Can you not just say it?" Parthiv persisted.

"I can but it is a habit to hold it in my hands. I like the rhythm of my saying it and moving my finger," Ramnik said. "Here let me show you how to do it."

"No dad, not now," Parthiv protested gently.

"Come on, give it a try. It won't bite you," Ramnik said.

Dipti looked at the father-son back and forth bemused as the snack sputtered and popped. Parthiv reluctantly went to his father to take the booklet.

"Okay, go to the first page and say it after me," Ramnik said and started reciting "Om bhur bhuva swaha…"

Parthiv started off well enough with Om and then went haywire with his pronunciation stretching the 'r' in bhur and making the 'bhu' sound like boo.

"Don't mock, son. This is a great language—Sanskrit. It is the world's most scientific language," Ramnik said.

"How come everything Indian is supposed to be only great, dad?" he asked.

"We never say that but Sanskrit is a truly great language. I don't say it. Many Western scholars would tell you that," Ramnik said.

Dipti picked up the first cluster of the snack with a strainer even as she felt pleasantly surprised by the generally temperate tone of Ramnik's response to Parthiv's mild defiance.

"You know when you say the Sanskrit consonants starting with the Ka sound and end with the Sa sound you can feel the sound traveling from your throat to the tip of your tongue. I was taught that in school," Ramnik said.

"That's cool dad but what do I do with it?" Parthiv said, not to challenge his father but out of genuine befuddlement.

"Not everything is about utility, Parth. Enjoy this great language, which once ruled India. I just want you to discover new things now that you are out of high school," Ramnik said.

Dipti interjected to say, "The breakfast is ready. You two come to the table." "Mama, can't the table come to me? I want to sit in the sofa and eat," Parthiv said.

"No, eating has a specific place. Besides, it is a nice family morning on Saturday. Let's have breakfast together," Dipti said.

Ramnik's mobile had a text alert.

"Can we talk privately?—Dhiru" it said.

Ramnik, sensing something amiss, replied, "Will call after an hour from the store." "Tks but don't forget," Dhiru said.

"Okay," replied Ramnik and settled down for breakfast.

There was a perceptible change in his mood that Dipti noticed immediately. "Who texted you?" she asked.

Ramnik kept chewing as if to postpone answering the question without lying.

He then took a sip of masala tea and said, "Oh, it was Jasu. Just asking how everything is."

Dipti said, "Oh, okay" but knew it was not Jasu. She decided not to press him and spoil the otherwise convivial family morning.

"So son, have you thought about what next? Which school would you like to go to? Are you going in for accountancy?"

"Not yet. I have been accepted at the College of Sunnyvale in business administration. I have not thought about accounting," he said.

"Business administration is good but accounting is more useful for our family business," Ramnik said. Even as he was saying that, he was grappling with his deviousness about keeping up the charade. He knew eventually Raghu Vishwa and the Sansthan would threaten to upset his plans.

Even if he managed to postpone the decision, he had to make it at some point in the not too distant future.

There were several factors weighing on him as he debated in his mind what course to take. One major factor was that Jasu had lent him $85,000 as a business loan a couple of years ago when his store had to be completely overhauled after he was served a notice under the California Retail Code. The notice listed six specific violations including, improper holding temperatures of potentially hazardous foods, improper cooling of potentially hazardous foods, inadequate cooking of potentially hazardous foods, poor personal hygiene of food employees, contaminated equipment and food from unapproved sources. His Patel-India Groceries also had a small eating joint subject to health department inspection.

He was ordered to refurbish the whole store to meet the code standards, compelling him to turn to Jasu for a loan. He had paid off $32,000 so far. He knew that Jasu had given him the loan both out of friendship and, equally, because they both followed the Sansthan. In recent months, it had become uncomfortably obvious to Ramnik that he may even have given the loan under urgings from Dhirubhai. A couple of months ago, when Jasu had come to pick up his monthly loan repayment check, he had said half in jest and half seriously that he would call the whole loan if he ever decided to go against the Sansthan.

Another factor playing on his mind was how it might play out within his community if he defied the Sansthan and not committed Parthiv to its lifelong service. He may yet manage to clear Jasu's loan and still do against the Sansthan but taking on the whole community seemed forbidding to him. Having grown up in India under parents who were unquestionably attached to the Siddhi order, Ramnik had struggled to chart his own independent course. His coming to America on a family green card had appeared to him to be a possible way out of that restrictive life but discovered soon enough that he and Dipti might even have chosen something even more confining. There were many occasions over the years when he had come close to disassociating from the Sansthan publicly. His lifelong conditioning by his parents had always pulled him back.

When Parthiv was born, both Ramnik and Dipti decided that they would have no more children. "Boy or girl, let's just have one child," Dipti had said when they first arrived in California. Always acutely conscious of the Sansthan, he reasoned that perhaps having just one son would give him the strength and resolve to stand firm when the time to commit him came. He thought losing the only son to the Sansthan would be so emotionally wrenching as to create in him unusual courage to turn the demand down. It may sound like strange logic but from his standpoint, it made perfect sense.

In contrast, Dipti was far more independent and clear. She was not necessarily opposed to the Sansthan with the uncharitable vehemence of Bela or quiet firmness of Jyoti. She believed the Sansthan served an important cultural and social purpose. However, the practice of virtually coercing families to give up their sons was abhorrent and had to be broken. If it meant breaking the practice with her son, so be it. More than anything else, one way or the other, Dipti wanted that to be a family decision and not something handed down as a Hobson's choice by the Sansthan and its operatives.

After breakfast, Ramnik told Dipti and Parthiv that he would go to the store for a short while. On his return, he had planned to go watch a movie of Parthiv's choice. Normally, Ramnik did not work weekends because he had hired someone else to manage the store but he did occasionally drop by to make sure things run smoothly. Dipti was not particularly surprised that he was going that morning but the text was playing at the back of her mind. Her woman's intuition told her that the text was from the Sansthan and likely from Dhiru. He was known to have done that in the past.

Patel-India Groceries was a modest size store not unlike other ethnic Asian stores on East El Camino Real in Sunnyvale. It was 2000 square feet. As it often happens with such stores, its name was a bit of a misnomer because it had become much more than a grocery store. It carried a wide range of products from India and South Asia. While food, spices, religious supplies and vegetables were the mainstay of the inventory in its early years, it had grown to sell clothes, shoes, Ayurvedic medicines, books and handicrafts. The inventory, although neatly arranged, had to be stacked up on one another because of the small size of the store.

The business was good until the notice from the state. It had set him back but in the past few months, things had begun to turn around, reviving Ramnik's plans to expand. He had decided that he would consider expansion only after he had paid off Jasu. He did not want to stretch the outstanding beyond 2014. The remaining $53000 meant he had to come up with about $4500 a month above his monthly income to settle the debt. Until June, 2014 he had averaged about $2000, adding to the backlog.

Jasu was pleasantly surprised that Ramnik had managed to increase the monthly from $1500. He had joked, "Ramnik, you seem determined to get the Sansthan off your back." Ramnik laughed but only nervously so. Ramnik had kept the loan from Dipti for a long time. It was just a week or so before Parthiv's graduation that he had finally told her about it. The disclosure caused considerable domestic tension with Dipti offering to sell off her jewelry to pay off Jasu.

"Jasubhai is good as long as you live up to his expectations. Once you fail, he is a different man. With this kind of indebtedness to him, he will suck the last ounce of our blood," Dipti had said on being told about the loan.

Dipti recognized that Ramnik had generally been an excellent provider and expeditious with his finance. He never ran up debts except the one he incurred because of the code violation notice. He kept her abreast of all financial details and together they maintained two joint bank accounts. He had no vices. His only major expense was that he loved big television sets, which he changed every year with advancing technology. His clothes came stitched from Shivabhai Tailors. Half a dozen pairs of shirts and trousers were parceled every year to him by Shivabhai along with a copy of the latest Hindu Panchang or almanac.

They had built up savings of $95,000 , which included a small portfolio of investment worth

$45,000 but he chose not to pay off his loan from that because it was on account of the business. He always knew that in case of an eventuality he could always draw from the savings and settle it. The turnaround in his business had convinced him that he was on course to clearing the debt soon.

Ramnik reached the store by 1 p.m. and had a quick chat with the manager about the sale so far. He then went to his office to call Dhiru.

"You said you wanted to talk privately. Is everything okay?" Ramnik asked.

"Yes, things are okay but I am a bit concerned about what the Sansthan and Swamiji are proposing," Dhiru said.

"What are they are proposing?" Ramnik said.

"You know how it is with Swamiji. It is never really a proposal but an order. When he proposes, it means it has to be done," Dhiru said.

"What has he asked you to do?" Ramnik said.

"Not just me but all ten of us. You know 2017 is the 55th death anniversary of our Guruji. Swamiji has told us all that we must initiate 55 monks by then to mark the anniversary," Dhiru said.

Ramnik took a deep sigh because he instantly knew what that meant.

"What this means is that we have to really step up our campaign to bring in new blood. I am worried about Parthiv," Dhiru said.

Ramnik fell into an abyss of silence. "Are you there Ramnik?" Dhiru asked.

"Yes, yes, I am just thinking," Ramnik said.

"There is not much time to think. 2017 is not that far," Dhiru said.

"You make it sound as if all this is cast in stone. You do know that none of this can be forced on anyone, right? We can always say no. As Dipti says, we decide what is best for Parthiv," Ramnik said.

"Of course, of course but you know there are implications to saying no," Dhiru said, careful not to make it sound like a threat. It was not.

"What's the worst that can happen? Some friends and family will end their relations with us. So what?" Ramnik said, surprising himself at his own courage. Some of Dipti's resolve had rubbed off on him.

"You know Ramnik we all have our own religious and spiritual obligations. It is not about what others say. It is about what you will say to yourself. Unfortunately, we all have mirrors in our homes," Dhiru said.

"Oh no, you are not going to take me on a guilt trip with you," Ramnik countered.

"I don't mean to. I am merely sharing my dilemma with you as an old friend. Swamiji has told me many times that he sees in Parthiv the kind of spark Guruji saw in Swamiji," Dhiru said.

"Swamiji has met Parthiv just a couple of times. I don't know how he sees whatever it is that he sees in him. In any case, these are not easy decisions and they have to be carefully thought through. Even though he is our son, we cannot presume to decide his future without his knowledge and consent," Ramnik said.

"And Swamiji agrees with that. He does not want to do anything against anybody's wish but we all have our own obligations. For those of us attached to it for so long, the Sansthan naturally takes precedence over individuals and their choices. The reason I wanted to talk to you today is because Swamiji is planning to be in Sunnyvale next week and he has expressed the wish to meet potential candidates together. Jasubhai has already agreed to send Jayendra. There are four others from Santa Clara and Fremont. You know Hemendrabhai, Rasikbhai , Charuben and Hiteshbhai's sons are also on the list of potential candidates. They will all be there," Dhirubhai said.

Ramnik was taken aback by the speed with which the recruitment campaign was moving. Even though he might have considered sending Parthiv to the Sansthan, he wanted to do it after college and that too for a couple of months to see if he liked it. There was no plan to expose him to the order so soon.

"It is very short notice. I have not even told Parthiv anything about it. He may sense something is going on but by no means does he think it has to do with him right away. I don't think we are ready to do it for the foreseeable future," Ramnik said.

Dhiru fell silent for a few moments. Even on phone Ramnik could sense that he was carefully weighing what he was about to say.

"You know the Sansthan has always stood by you, Ramnikbhai," Dhiru said.

"And I by the Sansthan. You should check my record of annual donations and the number of times I have sponsored trips by other swamis from India," Ramnik said.

"We are deeply grateful for that even though as devotees we owe it to our Guruji. You should never count what you give but should be grateful what you receive. You have received in return." Dhiru said, trying hard to skirt what he was about to say.

"What's that supposed to mean?" Ramnik asked in an aggressive tone. "I mean only generally," Dhiru said, still trying to zero in on specifics.

Ramnik knew that Dhiru specifically meant the loan that Jasubhai had given at the instance of the Sansthan. Dhiru knew that Ramnik knew what he was referring to without really naming it. Both were about to say it but both stepped back from the edge.

Before ending the call Dhiru said, "Think this over. I do not want to pressure you and Diptiben at all. We are coming only next Friday. There is enough time for you to have greater clarity. I cannot claim to know what it means for parents to willingly let their son go but I know what it feels to leave parents. I did it 35 years ago. I know the challenges but on the whole it has been a blessing for me," Dhiru said.

"We will talk again," Ramnik said.

He was strangely relieved now that it was all out in the open. Until now, there were only hints. He never liked interpreting hints. Having been a trader all his adult life, he preferred to be unambiguous and unequivocal. Selling meant he had to be specific and clear. Goods were sold, money was received. The obligation was met by the two concerned parties. He understood that world much better even though he had frequently dealt with the world of implied consequences that the Sansthan represented. He was unconsciously swiveling in chair when the store manager interrupted him.

"Ramnikbhai, Jasubhai is here," the manager said.

He thought to himself 'That was quick. These guys work in tandem.' He was wrong because Jasu did not know about Dhiru's call. He was visiting the store to pick up some supplies.

"I am here to get supplies for the meeting next Friday. I don't know if you have heard that Swamiji is visiting us. There will be a Rajbhog for about 300 people for two nights. As usual, it is on me to ensure that everything works well," Jasu said.

Ramnik feigned surprise and said, "Oh, I didn't know that. When was this decided?"

"This was confirmed only about an hour ago. Swamiji called me. He said he is going to call you as well," Jasu said even as Ramnik's mobile rang. It was from Raghu Vishwa.

"Namaste, Swamiji," Ramnik said, "Yes, I just found out from Jasubhai who is here at the store to get supplies for the Rajbhog."

"I have not been to the area for a long time. I thought it might be best to meet you all," Raghu Vishwa said.

"Our good fortune, Swamiji, that you are visiting us. Anything in particular I can do?" Ramnik asked.

"You are always generous in helping Jasubhai. I never have to tell you that anyway. I want to meet some of the boys during my visit. Why don't you bring Parthiv next Friday to the Sansthan Bhavan?" Raghu Vishwa said.

Ramnik was visibly disturbed by the request. Jasu noticed it but did not say anything. Ramnik was careful in not saying he would but merely that he would see him next Friday.

"Did he tell you bring Parthiv with you? Jayendra will be with me. It is always good for the boys to meet Swamiji. Don't you think?" Jasu asked, not really wanting to know whether he agreed but merely to rub it in because he had sensed Ramnik's reluctance.

"We will see. There is still time," Ramnik said.

"Do you expect the world to end before next Friday? What do you hope to see?" Jasu needled Ramnik.

"I mean it can end, can't it? But we will see what it means. Dipti and I will decide what is best for Parthiv," Ramnik said.

"You know you keep saying that as if the Sansthan is not best for him," Jasu persisted.

"You know Jasu, we have many other things to worry about. The Sansthan is there and we are happy it is there. I have no intention of going on and on about this. We have not made any decision yet. We may not make it any time soon. What you do with Jayendra is your and Jyoti's call," Ramnik said with unconcealed annoyance.

"Oh, let's not argue like last night again," Jasu said defensively as he realized that he had touched a nerve.

"And while we are on the subject, I will ensure that your loan is paid off before this year runs out," Ramnik said.

"Now that is not fair. Where is the connection between the two?" Jasu said. "You tell me, Jasu, you tell me," Ramnik said.

"You are still thinking about the joke I made the other day about the loan?" Jasu asked now fully aware that things were getting out of hand.

"Are you sure you were joking? You were 50% serious, I thought," Ramnik continued. "I am sorry you feel that way. I will never mix up the two—faith and money," Jasu said. Ramnik ordered a cup of masala tea for Jasu but by the time it came, Jasu had left.

CHAPTER 5

Ramnik spent a couple of hours more at the store, mainly trying to get his mind off the impending visit by Raghu Vishwa and Jasu's strangely unfriendly tone.

He called his personal banker to make sure his investments were in order. The banker, Peter O'Connor told Ramnik that his savings and investment portfolio together stood at $ 97,500 that morning. His investment in a tech company recommended by Bela's father Mahendra had gained some points in recent weeks. Ramnik had a fairly accurate idea about what he had in his accounts but hearing a specific number put his mind at rest. If it came to that, he could easily cut Jasu a check to settle the loan and shut up his unpleasant reminders.

The Patels still owed close to $60,000 on their mortgage and were conscious that offset against their savings and investment, they had barely $40,000 in total cash in hand. With the $53,000 still owed to Jasu, they were in effect in a financial hole by $13,000. It may not have been a large sum to tide over but Ramnik knew that everything depended on the revenues generated by the grocery store. Dipti would frequently express concern about what might happen were they to face an unexpected crisis. Ramnik tried to assure her by saying that with the rise in Indian population in the Bay Area his business could be expected to generate a steady flow. At the back of his mind though, he was equally concerned about their finances. That worry prompted him to keep track of their weekly receipts with anal attention. That explained why three store managers had quit in the last one year.

Before returning home, Ramnik asked the new store manager, 67-year-old Ravindra Jani who came courtesy of Jasu, about the sales for the week. They were $5820, including the $1675 that Jasu spent on purchasing supplies for the Sansthan event next week. As long as the store averaged gross sales of about $25,000 a month Ramnik knew that his finances would be stable. He expected that between the rest of Saturday and Sunday he would meet his target.

After paying for the inventory, store rent, utilities, manager, two helpers, insurance, and incidentals Ramnik managed to take home between $7500 and $9,000 monthly before taxes. After taxes he retained anywhere between $5000 and $7000, of which he paid a minimum of $ 2000 a month to Jasu. It was a tight balancing act month after month that meant that the Patels were never really fully comfortable. Life in the Bay Area was expensive and maintaining even a modest three- bedroom condominium in Sunnyvale cost him a monthly payment of $1850 on mortgage. In the end, they managed to save about $500 a month, which had added up to $95000 in about 20 years.

There were times when the receipts from the store dropped dramatically because of the fierce competition along East El Camino Real, which is dotted with Indian stores selling almost exactly the same inventory as Ramnik. The only differentiator was the kind of Indian fast food they served. However, even in that space there was little room to be innovative. There were times when Ramnik wondered how he managed to sell anything at all given that there were three Indian grocery stores within less than half a mile of his.

One important reason was that because of his affiliation with the Sansthan, many Sansthan followers felt obligated to shop at a store owned by one of their own. The importance of that sect- based fealty could not be overstated. Ramnik was very conscious of that and it influenced a lot of his socio-cultural conduct.

Back at home, Ramnik was greeted by Parthiv even though he was on phone with Bela. Dipti was watching the latest episode of "Teri Bindiya Mein Suraj Ki Lalima". Ramnik caught the central character of the soap, now in its fourth year, touching the feet of a man who did not even bother to look at her because he was busy peeling a banana.

Parthiv finished his phone call and turned to Ramnik, "Dad, I know you said we would go for a movie but may I go with Bela instead?"

Ramnik mocked disappointment with his face and said, "Sure, go ahead. I suppose you want me to drop you two."

Parthiv said, "Not two, three. Jayendra is joining as well. His mom will drop him here soon."

Ramnik said, "Okay. Tell me when you are ready." He went up to his bedroom to change while Dipti sat glued to the unfolding melodrama of "Teri Bindiya Mein Suraj Ki Lalima" where the old man whose feet the main actress was touching had kicked her to the accompaniment of drums.

As Parthiv waited for his friends to arrive, he sat next to Dipti. "Mom, why is that woman crying?" "Because her father-in-law kicked her," Dipti replied.

"What do you mean kicked her? How can he kick her?" Parthiv asked.

Putting her index finger on her lips Dipti said, "Parth, not now. I am watching."

"Mom, all episodes look the same to me. Tell me why he kicked her," Parthiv persisted.

"Because the meal she served was heated too much. It burned his tongue. So he is eating a banana to cool it down," she said.

Parthiv burst out laughing. "How does a banana cool a burned tongue?" Dipti did not answer and continued to watch.

"Mom, how does a banana cool a burned tongue?" he asked again. "I don't know Parth, it just does," she said in mild irritation.

Ramnik returned to the family room and asked Dipti, "Would you mind making me a cup of tea once your show ends."

Dipti said yes absent-mindedly because she was engrossed in the confrontation between the father-in-law and daughter-in-law who seemed to have gathered courage after years of having been mistreated and actually slapped him. The slap was shown from half a dozen angles with its echoes reverberating even as the credits rolled. A voiceover said, *"Sasur ke sehme gaal aur bahu ka thappad kya rang lata hai? Dekhiye agle Shanivaar raat aath bajey. (A chastened father-in-law and a daughter-in-law's slap. See what happens next Saturday at 8 p.m."*

The doorbell rang. It was Bela. Always cheerful, she greeted the Patels with great warmth. They both greeted her back and noticed that she wore a pair of short shorts and a tank top. Ramnik and Bela reflexively looked at each other. Both had Bela's clothes on their minds.

Jayendra came soon after with his mother Jyoti. He was dressed casually in a white T-shirt and denim shorts. Ramnik left with Parthiv, Bela and Jayendra while Jyoti decided to have a cup of tea with Dipti.

"I missed 'Teri Bindiya' because I had to bring Jay here. What happened today?" Jyoti asked.

"Oh, a lot of happened today. Do you want me to spoil it for you?" Dipti asked squeezing ginger in the tea pot.

Jyoti laughed and said, "Spoil? We have been at it for four years and it seems to have moved only an inch."

"Suhani (the central character) and Thakursaab (the father-in-law) had a major showdown. He kicked her first because the food was heated too much and it burned his tongue. And she finally snapped after years and slapped him," Dipti said.

Jyoti gasped and said, "Really? Slapped him? I don't believe it. Finally, revolution on Hindi television."

They both laughed and settled down for tea and some spicy puris. Jyoti suddenly became serious. She asked, "You heard, right?"

Dipti looking surprised, "Heard what?"

"That Swamiji is visiting next week," Jyoti said.

"No, I did not. Ramnik did not mention anything. May be because he just returned and went to drop the kids. What do you mean Swamiji is visiting next week?" Dipti said sounding alarmed.

"He is coming to Santa Clara and Fremont next Friday to Sunday. Jasu is ecstatic. He enjoys meeting Swamiji more than he enjoys sex with me," Jyoti said.

"I don't like this at all. I hope they don't expect us to meet," Dipti said.

"They do. In fact, Jasu is taking Jayendra. I am told Hemendrabhai, Rasikbhai, Charuben and Hiteshbhai's sons have also been called along with Parthiv,"Jyoti said.

"You have got me worried. I don't know why Ramnik has not told me yet. I am sure he knew it earlier," Dipti said.

"Jasu got to know this morning when Swamiji called him. He told me Swamiji spoke to Ramnikbhai too," Jyoti said.

Dipti looked upset at finding out about the visit from Jyoti. When Ramnik returned a half hour later, she confronted him in front of Jyoti.

"You did not think it important to tell me about Swamiji's visit and his calling Parthiv and others to meet him?" Dipti said.

Ramnink was not particularly perturbed. "I was going to tell you as soon as I returned but then I had to drop the kids at the theater. I am here now and I would have told you but it seems you already know."

Jyoti looked rather sheepish and said, "You know, let me go. I feel like I am causing tension."

Both Ramnik and Dipti said, "No, no not at all. Why should you feel bad? Please stay. It concerns us all."

The three sat down around the dining table.

"First, Jasu told me about Swamiji's visit and how he wants to meet some boys, including Parth. Then Swamiji called. He wants us to take Parthiv with us to the Sansthan Bhavan next weekend. I did not tell him that we would bring Parth with us. I kept it vague," Ramnik said.

Dipti turned to Jyoti and said, "What do you plan to do? I know you strongly disapprove."

Jyoti said, "I do but I have to choose my battles. I am thinking of letting Jasu take Jayendra this time. It is not like Swamiji is going to kidnap the boys with him next weekend. When it comes to the final decision, I will put my foot down. I have told Jasu he will have to choose between Swamiji and me."

Ramnik and Dipti were stunned to hear that. "Is it that bad between the two of you?" Ramnik asked.

"Over this issue, yes, because Jasu has lost his mind. I have seen how Jayendra uses abusive language more and more. He is rebelling. In fact, the other day he threatened to call the police if Jasu forced him to join the Sansthan. Jasu was about to slap him. I had to intervene and pacify them both. For me it is a particularly bad situation," Jyoti said.

"I am sorry to hear that, Jyoti. I sometimes think we may eventually have no choice in the matter. The way Dhirubhai and Swamiji talk you feel as if we gave birth to our sons only for the sake of the Sansthan," Dipti said with a wistfulness that surprised Ramnik a great deal because so far it was her who had been standing firm in her resolve.

"What happened Dipti that makes you say that? Is there something you are not telling me? Until last night, you were quite clear that it would be our decision even if we choose to commit Parth to the Sanshan. Until half an hour ago, you seemed perfectly normal watching that show. What has changed?" Ramnik asked.

"Nothing has changed. I still feel as strongly as I did last night but I was merely thinking aloud. I am quite conflicted because both you and I have spent our lives being so devoted to the Sansthan. I respect much of the work they do for Hindu culture. I don't even mind the idea of one son from a family joining as a monk. What I mind is the pressure they put on us," she said.

Jyoti was not sure if she heard it right. Did Dipti actually say she did not mind one son from a family joining as a monk? She wanted to press her on that but she had her own brewing crisis at home to deal with. Jasu had offered to drop Jayendra at the Patels for the movie but Jyoti came instead because she wanted to talk to them. She knew it was not possible to have a rational conversation with Jasu when it came to the Sansthan and Swamiji. Although the Patels were always as devoted to both like Jasu was, they never took an unyielding position.

Ramnik sat at the table drumming his fingers as if trying to harmonize his thoughts with the rhythm of his drumming. "I think we may all be overreacting. First of all, we still have some days before Swamiji arrives. A lot can change even in a few seconds. More importantly, as Jyoti said, it is not as if the boys will be taken under duress next week. There are ways to stall this," he said.

"You sound as if you have something dramatic planned before he arrives," Jyoti said.

"Not really. I am just pointing out how uncertain life is. As they say, let's cross the bridge when we come to it," he said.

All the reassuring philosophizing by her husband did not convince Dipti. "We have to be realistic, Ramnik. They will be here soon and they will soon demand that we make a decision. Whatever decision we make, it will have a deep impact on our lives. Don't you see that?" she said.

"I do see that but I also see other possibilities," he said. "Like what?" Jyoti asked.

"The Sansthan can always do with other kinds of help," Ramnik said. "You mean give them more money?" Dipti said.

"That is one way but I was thinking more about helping organize a fund-raiser for them," Ramnik said.

"You know they don't need money so much as they need monks. I think they have more than enough money. It is just that money is not buying them monks," Jyoti said.

"You know let's not spoil Saturday evening. Jyoti is here. Let's go shopping," Ramnik said, trying to change the subject.

"Shopping and me? Jasu looks at every bill these days. He keeps saying he has to recover all outstanding loans at the earliest," Jyoti said.

The last remark yet again came as a reminder to Ramnik. He was pretty sure Jasu had not discussed the loan he gave the Patels. How wrong he was in thinking that was proved almost immediately when Jyoti said, "He was saying something about an outstanding from you too. I did not know he had lent you money."

Ramnik involuntarily let a puff of disgust from his mouth. "You know Jasu is charging me a hefty interest; fourteen percent a year to be precise. I think this loan business has gone too far. I am going to settle it once and for all," Ramnik said.

Dipti was so stunned by the conversation that she practically ran upstairs. Ramnik went after her even as Jyoti apologized and left in a hurry saying, "I will pick up Jay from the theater directly. I am extremely sorry at the way this has turned out."

"Don't worry about it. It is not your fault," Ramnik said and went up.

Just as Jyoti started the car, her mobile rang. The ringtone was the Sansthan's familiar chanting of mantras. It was Jasu.

"Where are you?" he asked.

"I came to drop Jay at Dipti's. He has gone to watch a movie with Parth and Bela," she said. "When are you coming home? We have to talk about Jay and Swamiji," Jasu said.

"Listen Jasu, this is the limit. You are completely obsessed. I have told you what I feel. There is nothing to talk about. You make a choice—Swamiji and Sansthan or Jay and I," Jyoti said at the top of her voice and disconnected the phone.

Back inside the Patel home, Dipti and Ramnik sat next to each other without saying a word. It was very rare that Ramnik showed physical affection towards Dipti. He took her hand and clasped it in his hands.

After a minute or so, Dipti withdrew her hand and asked, "Do you think we can really pay off Jasubhai and still keep our finances in order? I don't think so. It is a simple calculation. We owe him 53,000. We owe 60,000 in mortgage still. Our savings are about 95000…"

"$97,500 as of this morning because our tech stock went up a bit," Ramnik interrupted her to correct as if that slight gain materially changed anything and helped quell Dipti's fears.

"We are in deep trouble, Ramnik. I don't know why you don't see it," she said and sobbed.

"We have some equity on the condo. The last time I check, we have about $23,000," Ramnik said, now struggling to find anything that might reassure Dipti. He knew Dipti had a history getting into a terrible panic and losing her emotional bearing in the process.

"Your optimism does not help. We have to be realistic. We have no real money. We cannot afford to antagonize the community. We cannot afford to antagonize the Sansthan or Swamiji or even Jasubhai, Really," she said.

Her clarity always irritated Ramnik but he knew she was right. Knowing that she was right and being acutely aware of their finances made him even angrier.

"I think we should consider taking Parthiv to meet Swamiji next week. We have to stay within the same community after all. We cannot antagonize them," she said.

"You have already said that once—not antagonizing the community. Don't keep repeating yourself," Ramnik said, his mood also becoming sour.

They both fell silent again until it was broken by Parthiv's call asking Ramnik to pick him up.

Ramnik got up to leave. Dipti said in an emotionally choked voice, "Don't tell Parth anything now. I will tell him next week."

CHAPTER 6

By the standards of Indian grocery stores, Patel-India Groceries was a reasonably efficient operation. The shelves were meticulously stocked and labelled. The carts were clean and their wheels all moved together in one direction without squeaking or being stuck. The isles were not sticky. The air-conditioning worked well. The store manager and staff were required to greet their customers. Clutter at the cash counters was frowned upon by Ramnik.

The only weak link, unbeknownst to Ramnik, was the main electric panel at the back of the store. The wiring was not up to code and the main switch was past its prime. It had maxed out its electrical load without anyone in the store realizing it. The manager, Ravindra Jani was a bank teller in India and had no aptitude for running an establishment like this. It took Ramnik a great deal of work to impress upon him the need to strictly adhere to the California Retail Code, whose violation under a previous manager had cost him $85,000 on overhaul.

When Ramnik added a couple of more freezers at the back of the store, he did not realize that the main switch had maxed out of on its load capacity. The store manager should have paid attention to such details but did not.

It was not surprising then that late on Sunday night, well after the store had been close, Ramnik was woken up by an urgent call from his store security's central room.

"Mr. Patel, We have a fire alarm at your store. The fire brigade is already at the site. You are urgently needed there," said an operator from the security company.

Ramnik woke up Dipti and said, "We have to go. There is a fire at the store."

Dipti, already reeling from her panic attack about their finances, complained that she had trouble breathing. Ramnik called Jasu and requested him to join him at the store and send Jyoti home to look after Dipti. He woke up Parthiv and asked him to accompany him.

They reached the store 15 minutes later by which time the fire caused by a short in the main switch and poor wiring had consumed about 45 percent of the space. There were half a dozen fire engines, three police cruisers and one ambulance. Ramnik went to the fire marshal and introduced himself. He asked him if he could go in.

"Sir, we cannot let you go until we have made sure the fire is fully put out. Was there anyone inside the store?" he asked.

"No sir, the store closes at 9 and no one is allowed after that," Ramnik said.

"I suggest you wait until we finish this. I will talk to you after that," the fire marshal said and went back to directing the firefighters.

Ramnik called Ravindra and asked him to come to the store immediately.

Jasu arrived ten minutes later. "This is so bad, Ramnik. How did this happen?"

"I also just got here. We don't know what happened. The fire marshal will look into that," Ramnik said and called Dipti.

She answered at the first ring. "Are you okay? Is Jyotiben with you?"

"I am okay and she is here. But what is going on at the store? We are ruined," she said.

"Can you please stop with your doom? I know we have a problem on hand. We will deal with it. For now, I am concerned about your breathing. Are you okay?" Ramnik said.

"Yes, Jyotiben is with me and I feel fine but very worried," Dipti said.

"Let's talk about that later. I have to go," Ramnik said and ended the call.

It took the firefighters over two hours to put out the fire. With electricity having been turned off, the store was dark except for the emergency lights. A mélange of foul odors emanated from the store, which were mostly like overcooked Indian food. The smells reminded Parthiv of James the jock's comment.

By the time the fire brigade completed the mopping up operations, it was 5.30 in the morning. The sun had begun to rise and the full extent of the disaster had begun to dawn on Ramnik. As it always happens with fires, water and foam often cause as much damage to the property as the fire. The first thing that Ramnik noticed was how the entire row of display coolers had practically burnt out. The two coolers closest to what seemed to be the source of the fire had partially melted. There were half charred packs of tandoori naans, puran polis, parathas, masala pizzas, patra, aloo samosas, okra, peas and containers of "kaju-kishmish" and "chikoo" ice cream. They all looked brutalized and caught unawares by the nightly fire.

At first glance, Ramnik recognized that all the perishable food had, well, perished. The displays closer upfront were all intact but fully soaked in foam and water. They looked perfectly fine but were, in fact, a total write off even if they were packed in polythene. Items such as salt, sugar, Indian spices, papad, wheat flour, Basmati rice, and a large variety of snacks looked undisturbed but now useless. Ramnik did try to make a quick determination if he could salvage any of the properly packed food items but them remembered the code violation fines and banished the thought.

Parthiv had fallen asleep in the car while Jasu was busy going through other isles. At one point the two, walking parallel in two adjoining isles met at the end. "This is terrible, just terrible," Jasu said trying to console. "I am so sorry. But don't worry we are there for you." Ramnik had a half smile, of the kind that is not really smile but facial distortion that mimics one under difficult circumstances.

Ravindra was in front at the cash counter, trying to restore some order. A police officer told him not to touch anything until the fire department had ruled out arson or deliberate fire. They were all asked to come out of the store.

Ramnik, Jasu and Ravindra waited near the main entrance as the police and what looked like a fire investigator went in.

"I think we had a problem of overload after we added those two new freezers," Ravindra said. Ramnik looked at him blankly and then said, "How do you know?"

"I noticed some lights flickering in the coolers and in the store room a couple of times. I thought I may even have heard some buzzing sound once while going in the cold storage," Ravindra said.

"Why didn't you tell me?" Ramnik asked, sounding alarmed.

"Oh, I thought it was just some power fluctuation," Ravindra said.

Ramnik took a deep sigh and walked off. He went to the car to check on Parthiv who was fast asleep. He called Dipti again.

"I will be here for a while. I am sending Parth home with Jasu. I will see you later," he said. "How bad is it?" she asked.

"Looks bad," he said and ended.

He requested Jasu to carry on and drop Parth on the way. "I can stay if you want," he said.

"Thank you but Ravindra and I are here. We will manage. You need to go to work too," Ramnik said.

"No I am off this week because of Swamiji's visit and the event," Jasu said.

Ramnik had totally forgotten about it because of the crisis on hand. "Well, we will not be able to attend anything now. We have a lot to deal with," Ramnik said.

"I understand, of course. I will tell Swamiji," Jasu said and left.

The fire marshal had returned by 9.30. He wanted to talk to Ramnik and Ravindra as a matter of routine.

"Our preliminary finding seems to suggest that your main electrical panel shorted. It looks like a very old switch and was probably badly overloaded. The wiring also does not appear to be up to code. The investigator thinks it was caused by overload. Once we make the final determination and if that finds code violation, you can expect significant penalty. We will let you know. It does not look like an arson action. For now you are free to get on with your cleaning up," the fire marshal said, shook hands and left.

"What about my insurance claim? Do I make it now or wait for your final report?" Ramnik asked.

"You will have to wait for the report because that will determine how this works out," the fire marshal said.

Ravindra was already inside unsure where to begin. Ramnik went in and surveyed the whole store and said, "I don't think I will emerge from this."

Ravindra held his head in his hands and began to weep. Ramnik called his banker O'Connor. "Peter, I need to see you right away. Are you at the branch?" he asked.

"Yes, I am Ram. Everything okay?" he asked solicitously.

"Nothing is okay. I will tell you when I see you," Ramnik said.

He told Ravindra to do what he can while he was going to meet the banker. Ravindra wiped his tears and said, "Ramnikbhai, I have some jewelry and some savings. You take it. This is my fault. I caused it." He broke down again. Ramnik went to him and put his hand on his back and said, "Don't blame yourself. We will see."

At the bank, O'Connor was waiting for Ramnik in the conference room. "Ram, what happened? You sounded so broken," O'Connor said.

"There was a fire at the store and I have lost everything," he said. O'Connor let out a soft whistle and asked, "Anyone hurt?"

"Fortunately not but the store is a total write-off," Ramnik said. "What about insurance?" O'Connor asked.

"That is going to be a problem potentially. The fire marshal said their initial finding suggests bad wiring and old electrical panel may have caused it. If that was indeed the case, then I may not get anything from the insurance," Ramnik said.

"I am so sorry to hear that. Please sit down. What can I do for you?" O'Connor said.

"I need to find out between my savings, investment and home equity, how much precisely I have and how soon I can get that," Ramnik said.

"Let's go to my cabin. I will have to get on the system," O'Connor.

They both settled down in O'Connor's office. After a few minutes, O'Connor said, "If we draw on everything, we are looking at about $ 120,000 give and take. We can process everything in a couple of days. Of course, your savings can be accessed right away."

"Okay. What about a line of credit?" Ramnik asked.

"That is possible against this collateral," O'Connor said.

"I will get back to you soon on which option I am taking. I want to be assured that a line of credit is an option," Ramnik said.

"It is. You have a clean record. So I don't see any problem there," O'Connor said.

Ramnik left the bank and went back to the store where Ravindra had already begun to clean up. He had called his son Soham to help. He told them that they should leave whenever they wanted and that he was heading home to catch some sleep.

Before leaving, he went to Isle 6. On the top shelf, which seemed fully dry, there were bell-shaped packs of golden yellow jaggery. He took one, opened it and scratched out bits. He ate a piece and gave one each to Ravindra and Soham.

As he sat in the car, his phone rang. It was from the Sansthan. Dhiru was calling.

"I am so sorry to hear about what happened. Jasubhai told me. We are fortunate that no one was hurt. How are you and Diptiben doing?" Dhiru asked with genuine concern.

"Thank you. We are okay but we have challenges ahead," Ramnik said.

"Let me know if I can do anything personally or the Sansthan can. Here speak to Swamiji," Dhiru said.

"Ramnikbhai, I am so sorry at your loss but happy that no one was hurt. The Sansthan is always behind you. Do not hesitate to ask us," Raghu Vishwa said.

"Thank you, Swamiji. I appreciate it. I am glad you care. I wanted to tell you that we will not be able to make it next week when you are here. Just too many ends to tie up now," Ramnik said.

"Oh, it goes without saying. Don't worry about it. We can always meet some other time. You know you can call me at any time. Please don't worry. Namaste," Swamiji said and ended.

CHAPTER 7

Ramnik reached home around 2 p.m. Tired, groggy and famished, he first went to take shower. Fortunately, Dipti was asleep. Parthiv too was asleep in his room.

The shower did him a world of good. He believed that water oxygenated the body in such a way that it felt reborn. However, he also knew that that feeling was generally short-lived. One could be lulled into complacency by a good, long shower.

With the home quiet, he came down to the kitchen where Dipti had kept a full meal ready. She had made her favorite—okra sprinkled with spiced up gram flour, Tuver Dal with peanuts, shredded carrot raita, lightly fried chash with a generous sprinkling of coriander, finely cut radish leaves with a dash of oil, hing and salt, papad and rotli. There was Dipti's famous sukhdi, made from jaggery and wheat flour. It seemed the food had been recently warmed up. He saw a note on the kitchen island. It was from Jyoti. It said, "It is 1.30 and I am leaving. I have left your food. I gave Dipti some relaxant and she is asleep. She might take a couple of hours to wake up. Will talk later."

By the time he finished his lunch, it was 3 p.m. He went back to his bedroom and fell asleep next to Dipti. It was only around 6 p.m. that a gentle tapping on his shoulder woke him up. It was Dipti, "It is 6. Would you like to wake up now? I am making tea. Parth is awake too. We can have dinner soon."

Ramnik did not say anything but went to the bathroom to freshen up. Coming down the stairs, he heard the doorbell ring. He opened it and found Bela with her father Mahendra and mother Meena.

"Welcome, Mahendrabhai, Meenaben. Please come. We were just about to have tea," Ramnik said. The four adults went to the family room. Bela and Parthiv went to his room.

"I did not call because I knew you would be busy and thought it might be best to visit you. How bad is the damage to the store?" Mahednra asked.

"I would say about 45% gutted by the fire and the rest badly damaged by the firefighters extinguishing the fire. I will have to write off the whole inventory. That is about $45,000 or so," Ramnik said. "Also, the five coolers have been destroyed. That is another $15,000 or so. I am sure there will be other unforeseen expenses and losses that will add up. We are looking at a total wipeout."

Dipti had already begun to cry with Meena trying to pacify her. "Diptiben, please don't cry. What are we here for? You will come out of this," she said.

"What about insurance? Is that in order?" Mahendra asked.

"It is in order but what the fire marshal said has got me worried. He said their initial finding suggested that the main electrical panel and the wiring were not up to code. That could create problems for the insurance. It all depends on what their final report is. In my mind, I am ready for the worst. I have to be ready with about $150,000 if I want to get back on track," Ramnik said.

"Do you have any equity on the condo?" Mahendra continued with his matter-of-fact questions.

"We do but all told, including the savings and investment, I can pull about $125,000. That will put us deep into debt. It would be like starting our lives all over again," Ramnik said and for the first time his eyes welled up.

Mahendra got up and rubbed his back. "Listen, I am here to help in any way I can. You should not worry about the money. Fortunately, we have reserves. Tell me what the final amount is and I will transfer it," Mahendra said.

"That is so generous of you but I cannot accept it. It is too much money and I will not be able to pay it back for a long time," Ramnik said.

"Don't worry about repayment. We will talk about it when the time is right. For now, do not draw from your savings or portfolio. You have to think about Parth's future too," Mahendra said.

Ramnik fell silent. He seemed to be lost in deep thought. After a couple of minutes, he said, "May be this is a signal."

"Signal? From whom?" asked Mahendra.

"Signal that I need to pay more attention to the Sansthan. You know I managed to escape becoming a monk because of my TB. Perhaps this is my punishment for that. It all catches up right here," Ramnik said, almost breaking down.

Mahendra was taken aback by the sudden change of mood. Ramnik looked like a different man. It was as if there was a dramatic change of personality. He thought perhaps it was just the nerves acting up now that the sense of loss was sinking in.

What appeared to have compounded Ramnik's plight was the very real possibility that the insurance company may not accept the claim if it resulted from negligence. There was also the question of the insurance wanting to establish if it was a deliberate fire. All this was routine investigation that could delay the claim settlement, if it took place at all. Mahendra was disturbed to hear that the fire marshal had expressed misgivings about the main electrical panel and wiring. Given Ramnik's earlier problems with the California Retail Code, he had a rough slog ahead.

Dipti and Meena came out with tea and snacks. They both froze in their tracks when they say saw Ramnik wiping his tears. Dipti hurriedly kept the tray down and rushed to Ramnik. "Are you crying? Why are you crying? Are you hiding something from me?" she asked rapidly.

Mahendra intervened and said, "He is naturally emotional and stressed out. Things are going to be fine. We can work together on this."

Ramnik looked up and looked at Dipti. He seemed rather out of sorts. "Dipti, this is a signal." Dipti was confused to hear him talk that way. She asked Mahendra, "What is he saying?"

Mahendra said Ramnik was feeling distraught and had to rest. Dipti said she had some relaxant, which she had taken earlier. She went up to fetch the medicine. Mahendra tried to soothe Ramnik's frayed nerves but to no avail. He kept saying "This is a signal."

Hearing the commotion both Bela and Parthiv came down. They did not understand what was going on. Parthiv went to his father and asked, "Dad, what is happening? Why are you looking so strange? Are you okay?"

Ramnik looked at Parthiv and flashed a non-committal smile. He said nothing. Dipti brought the medicine and a glass of water. Ramnik took the pill somewhat reluctantly and stretched on the sofa.

"I think you should go to your bedroom and rest, perhaps sleep the tension off. I am sure you will feel fine in the morning tomorrow. May be you should eat some and then call it a day. A lot has happened since last night," Mahendra said.

Ramnik did what was suggested and went up to his room. Half an hour later, he had fallen asleep.

Mahendra and Meena kept Dipti company for a while. They all decided not to discuss what had transpired. Instead, Dipti switched on the TV in time for the next episode of "Teri Bindiya Mein Suraj Ki Lalima".

Meena said, "You watch it too? I do too. Did you see what happened yesterday? Suhani slapped Thakur. Serves him right."

The show's theme song had just begun to play when Dipti switched on the TV. "Nooooo, not that again," Parthiv said in mock anger as Bela chortled.

Mahendra, who had brought his iPad, decided to do some company work as the two women got busy with the soap. It opened with the repeat of the resounding slap from various angles before one of the cameras finally dissolved to Thakur smarting under the impact of the slap. The slap was not as hard as the humiliation it caused and the way it instantly reversed domestic balance that was always heavily tilted in his favor being the man of the house and a retired feudal lord.

Bela and Parthiv decided to sit in their small backyard. Both were conscious that despite the appearance of some normalcy having returned, there was obviously going to be a long-term problem. Neither fully understood the full measure of the financial challenge that Ramnik faced but his breakdown suggested to them that things were far from good.

"Did you hear how he kept telling mom that it was a signal," Parthiv asked.

"Yes but I don't know what that meant. First I thought his mobile was not working properly," Bela said and laughed.

Parthiv seemed distracted and even worried. He finally said, "I think dad is in serious financial trouble because of the fire. He thinks it happened because he did not do something that Dhiru uncle asked him to do."

"What do you mean?" Bela asked.

"I don't quite know but I think it has to do with Swamiji. I think that is what it is," Parthiv said.

After a few minutes, they both went in to eat. Dipti and Meena were still watching the last few minutes of the "Teri Bindiya Mein Suraj Ki Lalima". This time, half a dozen others had gathered in the cavernous living room of the grand mansion, each wearing an expression of disgust and anger. A woman, who seemed like the matriarch of the family, was fanning herself. Parthiv caught that sight and asked, "Why is that old woman fanning herself, mom? Don't they have air-conditioning in this palace?"

Dipti did not answer.

After the episode ended Dipti, Mahendra and Meena ate dinner at the dining table. The two kids had already finished theirs. Half an hour later, by 10.30 the Amins had left. Dipti cleaned the kitchen, loaded up the dishwasher and went up after switching it on. As she was going up, she saw Parthiv sitting and staring at the ceiling.

"Parth, what is it? Are you okay?" she asked.

"Yes mom, just thinking about dad. He looked weird when he kept talking about some signal. I hope he feels better tomorrow," he said.

"He sure will. Otherwise, I am going to call Swamiji," she said. "What can he do?" Parthiv said.

"I think he can calm him down and reassure him," she said and went to her bedroom.

CHAPTER 8

Raghu Vishwa having long gone to bed, Dhiru finally had some time for himself at Bear Valley. Monks at the Sansthan were allowed to watch television as long as it was "wholesome and positive". Dhiru had been around long enough with the Sansthan to be the de facto number 2 man of its U.S. operations. Among the privileges he had was a television in his bedroom. He was not particularly fond of entertainment. He mainly watched documentaries. Flipping channels, he chanced upon one. By a strange coincidence, it was a new documentary about how Indian spiritual and yoga gurus had deeply influenced America.

The documentary had a passing reference to the Sansthan, particularly Guruji and his association with the portrait photographer called Kevin Church. Dhiru had not seen the documentary before and what he was about to come across would unsettle him. In establishing how Indian gurus and yogis had captured the popular imagination in America for a long time, the documentary titled "And the Ganga flows through America" included Church as one of the many examples. Curiously enough, while it was largely positive about Church's association with Guruji, it mentioned a couple of diary entries toward the end of the photographer's life where he was quoted as expressing serious disillusionment about "forcing young men into a life of celibacy against their wishes."

The documentary showed excerpts from Church's handwritten entries with the voiceover saying, "Among the more controversial practices of the

Indian spiritual-industrial complex is the way some of the institutions bring in young men as novice monks to their fold. As Kevin Church's diary entries suggest this is not a new practice. Church, an accomplished portrait photographer who spent his entire life from the 1940s until his death in 1981 in India, left some troubling questions behind."

There was a brief interview with Tapeshwar Vishwa, the swami who looked after the Sansthan's Haridwar ashram. Tapeshwar Vishwa, sitting by the flowing Ganga behind him, said in Hindi, "सिद्धि प्राप्ति संस्थानने कभी भी कककिको उनकी इच्छा के विरुद्ध कदम लेनके लिए विशि नहं ककया। जो भी हैं ण हमारे थिय है बि ह ह्हन्दू मिमम की अत उत्तम प्रथाओं को ध्यान में रख हुए हमारे थिय जुडे हैं। मुझे नहं प की श्रीमान के नि चचम ने क्या देखा लेककन हमारे गुरूजी भारत की श्रेष्ठ परंपरा के तकि हैं ।" (Siddhi Prapti Sansthan has never compelled anyone to go against their wishes. All our monks are with us out of their commitment to the highest ideals of Hindu religion. I do not know what Kevin Church said he saw but guruji is a symbol of the best in Indian traditions."

The documentary was generally a positive chronicle of its chosen theme. What concerned Dhiru was that in trying to point out some of the so-called weaknesses the documentary maker had specifically focused on the Sansthan and even showed shots of the Bear Valley ashram. He was not sure who authorized the filmmaker to shoot within the campus because all such requests would have been referred to him by Raghu Vishwa. Although the tone of the bit about the Sansthan was not predominantly negative, he was troubled that an idea about coerced initiation of monks had been put out on American television. It was a potentially serious matter but not serious enough for him to have woken up Raghu Vishwa at 11.30 at night.

He had a disturbed sleep that night and woke up by 4 a.m. the next morning to coincide with Raghu Vishwa's routine. Although Dhiru normally woke up at 6 a.m., he felt it important enough to bring the documentary to Raghu Vishwa's notice.

"You are up early today. How come?" Raghu Vishwa asked him as he began perambulating around the inner circle of the ashram.

"It is a matter of some importance, Swamiji," Dhiru said. "Do tell. What is it about?" Raghu Vishwa asked.

"I happened to watch a documentary last night called 'And the Ganga flows through America'. It was generally about how Indian gurus and spiritual masters have influenced America…." He said and was interrupted by Raghu Vishwa.

"I know about it. Tapeshwarji had told me about his interview regarding Kevin Church. It is nothing important," Raghu Vishwa said.

Somewhat relieved Dhiru said, "Then I suppose you also know about how they used some outside shots of the ashram."

That surprised Raghu Vishwa. "That I did not know. We have not authorized anyone. How did they get those? Not that we would have refused permission had they asked," Raghu Vishwa said.

"I don't know, Swamiji. I did not authorize anyone," Dhiru said.

"Now that is a cause for concern. Do you think someone from among us supplied it?" Raghu Vishwa asked.

"I cannot say for sure but it looks that way," Dhiru said.

"Someone with an ulterior motive perhaps?" Raghu Vishwa said. "Hope not. Let me find out today. I will get back to you," Dhiru said.

"You do that and be careful not to accuse anyone without being certain. We don't want any adverse publicity. We have a visit coming up this week to the Bay Area. We are meeting some potential donors and those boys too," Raghu Vishwa said.

"I know Swamiji. I will be discreet," Dhiru said.

"Since you are here, let me tell you to call Ramnikbhai during the day. I would like to talk to him," Raghu Vishwa said.

"Sure, Swamiji," Dhiru said and went to his office.

His was the only office with computers and broadband connection. There was another set of PCs with internet connectivity but they were in the library and under password protection. The monks were allowed to use them but their requests had to be approved by Dhiru.

Tea and coffee were strictly prohibited on the ashram campus. Dhiru kept a copper pitcher to store water. He drank from it from time to time. He sat down in his swivel chair and began thinking about who could have supplied the footage. Having practically run the U.S. operations on behalf of Raghu Vishwa for close to 30 years he knew every staffer and monk personally. He began sizing up people with access of the kind that would be needed to film. After 15 minutes of process of elimination, he made a list of four people, two monks and two lay staff. The lay staff included Hemendra Joshipura, an accountant, and Keshubhai Randeria, a general manager. Both had access to all the storerooms and inventories, including all ashram keys. The monks on the list were Kirti Vishwa and Trymbak Vishwa. Both were senior monks with unfettered movement around the ashram. These were not necessarily "suspects" but those who might know if someone was filming. Going by the quality of the footage it was not undercover or surreptitious but done with proper lighting and angles.

Dhiru was called by Raghu Vishwa to his office around 10 a.m. for their morning meeting to take stock of U.S. activities. Before getting on with that business, Raghu Vishwa asked Dhiru, "Have you any names for me?"

"I do Swamiji. I am not at all saying they did it but they are the ones with most access and they might have known or seen something," Dhiru said and gave the four names.

"Okay. Also, get in touch with the documentary maker to find out how he got the footage. We will see how this goes. Now, let us call Ramnikbhai. I was told yesterday by Jasubhai that things are not good," Raghu Vishwa said.

Dhiru called the Patel residence. Parthiv answered.

"Beta, may I speak to your father. Swamiji would like to talk to him," Dhiru said. "Dad is at the store," Parthiv said.

Dhiru told Swamiji that.

In the meantime, Dipti came to the living room and on seeing Parthiv on phone asked, "Who is it?" "It is Dhiru uncle, mom," he said.

She took the phone from Parthiv and said, "Dhirubhai, I am glad you have called. I was going to call you because I wanted to speak to Swamiji."

Unsuitable Celibate?

"Why? Well, he is right here and he wanted to talk to Ramnikbhai," Dhiru said.

"He is at the store but before you speak to him, let me speak to Swamiji please," she said.

Dhiru hesitated before he said, "I know these are difficult circumstances for your family. But we have to respect the traditions of the Sansthan. Swamiji would not be able to speak to you directly. You know he does not interact with women directly. I can convey to him whatever you want to."

In her troubled state, Dipti had forgotten about the strict observance of "No contact with women" tradition of the Sansthan. The only time someone had tried to break that was when Ramnik's cousin Ela Sheth had addressed him directly and called him a "masquerader" hiding an insidious agenda of "real estate and money-grabbing" behind spirituality. Even then, Raghu Vishwa has chosen not to engage her and walked from the fundraiser.

"Tell Swamiji that Ramnik is deeply disturbed. I don't know why he has gone to the store. You need to speak to him right away. He needs help. He is a broken man," Dipti said.

"Swamiji says he will call him on his mobile. Leave it to us. We will take care of it," Raghu Vishwa said.

The next call went to Ramnik who was sitting in his office at the store and staring at the ceiling.

He answered the phone.

"Ramnikbhai, Swamiji here. Listen, I have been keeping track of everything that is going on. We are with you 100 percent. The Sansthan always stands by its supporters, no matter what. I am coming this Friday. I know you are busy but let's meet," Raghu Vishwa said.

"It was my fault Swamiji. This is the punishment for that. The fire was a signal. I could not become a monk because of TB. Parth should become one," Ramnik said.

Raghu Vishwa was not sure if he heard it right but said, "Listen, wait until this Friday. We will talk. The Sansthan does something for you. You do something in return," he said and ended the call.

CHAPTER 9

A glistening rust orange color Mercedes Sprinter pulled up under the canopy entrance of the Sansthan Bhavan in Sunnyvale. About two dozen men waited with marigold garlands as Dhiru alighted from the driver's seat after opening the sliding door on the passenger side.

The door opened as if its speed was timed so as to reveal its occupant in a dramatic fashion. As the waiting men saw the widely smiling face of Raghu Vishwa, there was an audible gasp. At least two men at the head of the throng prostrated on the asphalt floor. Raghu Vishwa, who was someone long accustomed to such abject deference among his devotees, betrayed no awkwardness. He stood there for a few seconds blessing the men with both his hands. Among the men was Ramnik who waited at the back of the crowd.

Raghu Vishwa walked in as if he was levitating on the reverence of his followers, some of whom may not even have minded carrying him on their shoulders. By the time he entered, there were about 15 garlands around his neck. It appeared as if he had a bunch of garlands for a beard.

Dhiru took Jasu aside and said, "Swamiji would have a light lunch and then he would like to rest for a couple of hours."

Even a request as mundane as that had the effect of an electrifying command on Jasu who vigorously shook his head in agreement. He had to do nothing at all to facilitate Raghu Vishwa's lunch and subsequent rest but the way he charged ahead of Swamiji it seemed as if nothing would happen without his intervention.

A round dining table, seating six, was ready with freshly cooked food. The familiar aroma of pure desi ghee wafted from a small hill of jeera rice in a large plate. Around the rice, there was an assortment delicious vegetarian food. The Sansthan cook, who had been instructed three times by Jasu in the morning to take a thorough bath, had made Raghu Vishwa's favorite "adad ni chhooti dal' and "bharela bataka". After washing his hands in a silver bowl held by Jasu with water being poured from a pitcher by Ramnik, Raghu Vishwa sat down for lunch. Dhiru sat opposite him while the rest just stood a few steps away.

Raghu Vishwa was a light eater. He had a couple of small spoons of "adad ni chhooti dal', "bharela bataka", one rotli and little rice. He ended the meal with vagareli chash, another favorite; although in recent years he had more or less given up fried food.

The lunch wrapped up, Raghu Vishwa retired to his room as his aides and confidants settled in the main waiting area to plan for the event on Saturday. Friday was kept relatively free. Once the Saturday event was finalized, Dhiru took Ramnik to a separate office. Jasu noticed that he had been kept out but he could do nothing about it.

"How are you Ramnikbhai? I am worried about you," Dhiru said.

"I am okay but trying to solve my problems. You know that the insurance company is likely to reject my claim," Ramnik said.

"I did not know that. How much claim did you make?" Dhiru said.

"100,000 but my loss seems a little more than that. They said the fire department's report pointed out an old electrical panel and some wiring issues, which may have caused the fire. They may reject it on that ground but I am waiting for the final report," Ramnik said.

"Do you have enough savings to cover the immediate costs," Dhiru asked.

"I do but once I use that I will be left with nothing. The fire has given us a bad reputation and I don't know whether I will regain customers. The other stores are already grabbing them," Ramnik said.

"The Sansthan can help you there. We have some 10,000 followers in this area. We can appeal to them to stand by your store. Of course, that appeal cannot be open and direct. We have to be tactful about it. We are a not for profit institution and we cannot indulge in anything that would have an adverse effect on our status. The IRS watches all such Indian institutions very closely," Dhiru said.

Ramnik fell silent. He kept staring at the desk. Dhiru noticed his change of mood and said, "You went missing, Ramnikbhai. Don't think so much. It is a loss but not such that you can't ever overcome. If it comes to that I will give you a loan."

For someone who had been assured by two friends of a loan or investment without any collateral, Ramnik showed a worrisome depressive streak. While Bela's father Mahendra had gone so far as to say he would transfer the loss amount, Dhiru also promised an interest-free loan. Yet, there was nothing in Ramnik's demeanor to suggest that reassurance.

"Is there something else that is troubling you, Ramnikbhai?" Dhiru asked.

"No, it is just I have been thinking about how I could have been what you are. But for my TB, I would have ended up as a monk. My parents were all set for that," Ramnik said.

"Yes, but that is an old story. You should not dwell on the past because it is not productive," Dhiru said.

There was a tap on the door. It was Jasu. "Swamiji is awake and he has asked for you," he said. Dhiru left immediately.

"Ramnikbhai, are you alright? We are all there for you," Jasu said.

"I know, I know and I am so grateful. I am going to stop worrying about the store. Everything will be okay," he said.

The two of them went back to the living area and joined the other men in talking shop. Word had already spread about the fire at Ramnik's store. There were some solicitous inquiries but other than that, not much transpired. Half an hour later, Dhiru came out to call Ramnik and Jasu inside.

"Swamiji wants to see you both," he said.

They all removed their shoes at the door and went into the bedroom. Raghu Vishwa was sitting on a sofa upholstered in red faux silk fabric. Ramnik and Jasu touched Raghu Vishwa's feet and sat on the floor.

"Dhirubhai told me that he spoke to you at length. I want to assure you that the Sansthan will help you in any way it can. So please forget about your worries now," Raghu Vishwa said.

Finally, Ramnik smiled. Not to be left out, Jasu smiled even wider. "I told him, Swamiji, that Swamiji is will take care of everything," he said.

"Now let's talk about tomorrow. How many boys are you bringing?" Vishwa asked Jasu. "All, Swamiji, all. Jayendra is very excited," he said.

Vishwa turned to Ramnik and asked, "Are you bringing Parthiv?" Ramnik said he was not sure but he would try.

Saturday's event was at Yoga Sthanam, a smaller hall with a stage next to the living area. Since it was meant only for the six boys and their fathers the arrangements were not elaborate. There was an ornate throne like chair on the stage where Raghu Vishwa sat. In front of him on the floor, a couple of red carpets were spread out. The boys sat on the right hand side carpet and the fathers and other male functionaries on the left. The three sons of Hemendra, Rasik and Hitesh were brought by their fathers. Jasu came with his son Jayendra as well as Charu's son because being a woman she was not allowed to attend. She decided to wait in the car in the parking lot.

Raghu Vishwa quickly surveyed the gathering and registered the absence of Ramnik and Parthiv. He began by chanting the Gayatri mantra and then ended the recitation with the Guru mantra. His eyes remained shut a few seconds after he had finished. The five boys sat there looking generally disinterested with Jayendra checking Facebook updates on his iPhone hidden in the well of his folded legs. He had managed to say on his status "At the temple. WTF? Why am I here listening to this bullshit?" There were already half a dozen likes on it.

Raghu Vishwa opened his eyes and said, "Life is not only Facebook and WhatsApp status updates." That spooked Jayendra out even though Swamiji had just made a general comment. Raghu Vishwa did not know that Jayendra was posting. That is when Ramnik and Parthiv walked in. Ramnik touched his head at the edge of the stage, while Parthiv bowed towards Raghu Vishwa and said 'Namaste'. He sat next to Jayendra who whispered, "Hey dude, tsup?"

"Okay now that we have everyone let me say a few things. As I was saying, life is not only Facebook and WhatsApp updates. I know it seems fun for you but it serves no purpose other than giving you momentary happiness. The real happiness comes when you lead a life that is anchored into the deep and serene ocean that is Indian culture and traditions. There is a reason why I have called you here. You are the chosen ones…." Vishwa said.

He was interrupted by Jayendra who said, "Chosen for what?"

Jasu was finding it hard to contain his anger at his son's behavior but could not do anything because he did not have courage to violate the Sansthan's rules—when Swamiji speaks, none else can.

Raghu Vishwa sternly looked at Jasu and then turned to Jayendra. In that brief movement, his expression had turned into a picture of amiability. Jasu knew he was not happy at being interrupted but Jayendra was treated very differently.

"There is a word in Hindi called Utavla. It means impatient. Impatience is a destructive emotion. You must know how to wait in life. You are the chosen ones to lead a life of nobility and higher purpose. I know this may not make sense for you youngsters but you will soon understand," Vishwa said.

He then gave the boys a quick overview of the Sansthan and why it was important that people supported it. He also briefly touched upon the importance of restraint but avoided celibacy. After a 15-minute presentation, Raghu Vishwa said, "You may ask any questions."

"Can we leave now?" Jayendra asked as the others laughed, Parthiv only awkwardly so.

"You may leave any time you want. There is no compulsion at the Sansthan," Raghu Vishwa said flashing his trademark beatific smile. He turned towards Jasu again and looked at him blankly.

"I have a question, Swamiji," said Parthiv.

Ramnik became alert and anxious, not knowing what he might ask.

"Why did you join the Sansthan and when?" Parhiv said. Jayendra looked at his friend in disgust and said the F word without saying it out loud followed by "Really?!"

"I am so glad you asked Parthiv. I joined when I was almost your age. Guruji took me under his wing. That was a long time ago. It was in 1956. I joined because I had no family, no parents. I was wasting time in Haridwar when Guruji saw me. Since then I have been here," Raghu Vishwa said.

With no more questions coming up, the meeting ended. The boys touched Raghu Vishwa's feet with Jayendra barely bending. As the gathering began to disperse, Raghu Vishwa told Parthiv, "Come visit us at the ashram sometime."

Parthiv just smiled. Jayendra and Jasu left together. Their body language suggested clear tension between them. As the exited the building, Ramnik could see through one of the glass windows Jasu slapping Jayendra and Jayendra smashing his phone on the ground. Had it not been for Charu's intervention, things might have gotten worse.

Ramnik and Parthiv left half an hour later. They were both in a reflective mood. Driving back, Parthiv said, "Dad, I liked it."

CHAPTER 10

The content of the letter from Sunlight Insurance was predictable. It cited the fire department's initial report about the old electrical panel and bad wiring as the ground for their turning down Ramnik's claim of $100,000.

> *"Dear Mr. Patel,*
>
> *We are in sympathy with you on account of your business being damaged by a fire. Sunlight Insurance processes all such claims with complete diligence. After examining your claim and making onsite inspection, we are unable to grant you your claim at this time. If there is anything else we can do, do not hesitate to contact us. Thank you for your business.*
>
> *Rebecca Rowling*
> *Senior Claims Officer*
> *Sunlight Insurance"*

Ramnik read the letter twice as if the second time around it may change its content. Sitting in his store, he kept staring at the ceiling. He then called Rebecca Rowling.

"Ma'am, I am calling to request a review of your claim denial. The electrical panel and wiring were not as bad as being made out. There was never any problem. I have paid my premium unfailingly for 20 years. I have paid in excess of a quarter million dollars without ever claiming any benefit. Now that I have a desperate need you are turning me down," he said.

Rowling heard him out patiently and said, "Sir, we have to go by the report of the fire department. It is their preliminary finding. If they change it, we would more than happy to settle your claim. We know you have been an excellent customer but we have to follow the rules and policies. I suggest we wait until the final report."

"How long should I wait?" Ramnik asked.

"As soon as the fire department issues its final report. It is not in our hands. I am sorry," she said. Realizing that he was not going to get anywhere with the claims officer, he decided to end the call.

Ravindra came into his office and said, "I have gone through the inventory. We can salvage a lot of it. The dals and snacks are all in plastic bags. They have not been affected at all. There are a lot of other things that we can clean up and if the need be offer at a discount."

Ramnik was still preoccupied with the rejection from the insurance company. He absent-mindedly said, "What?"

Ravindra said it again. Ramnik explained that given their earlier problems with the health authorities, it would too risky to sell anything from the stock even if it was perfectly clean.

Ravindra asked what if they sold it with a clear notice that the inventory was salvaged from fire. Ramnik had zoned out again. After a few seconds he said, "What was that?"

Ravindra realized the futility of his suggestion and said, "Nothing. I agree."

It took them another two weeks to clean the store fully, change the electrical panel and replace the old wiring with new. With insurance claim not coming through, Ramnik had to pay by selling some of his stocks much against the advice of Mahendra. By the time he finished restoring the store to normal, he had spent an upward of $55,000, much less than he had anticipated. One way he had saved on the expense was by reducing the size and variety of the inventory. He had decided not to carry clothes, books and handicrafts. Ravindra had managed to sell the clothes and handicrafts from the pre-fire stock at a heavy discount of 45 percent. What would have been a total write-off had earned Ramnik about $10,000. They had also managed to sell most of the food inventory to friends by taking waivers from them. The total proceeds from the fire sale were $18,000. As a gesture for his efforts, Ramnik had given Ravindra a commission of $1800.

Six months after the fire, Ramnik's business had stabilized again. He had called Rowling at Sunlight to tell her that he was canceling the insurance because of the way he had been treated. He had also added for good measure that the ten or so Indian businesses, which he had switched to Sunlight on his recommendation, had also decided to take their insurance business elsewhere. That got Rowling's attention because together it meant a loss for Sunlight of a monthly premium totaling about $20,000.

"Why don't we all meet before you take the final decision? I can come out there whenever you want," she said, Sensing an opportunity, Ramnik decided to hold off cancellation until the meeting. The meeting was set for a week from then. Before that, a letter from the fire department bolstered his confidence. It had cleared him of any wrongdoing and, in fact, said the electrical panel in question was still within code time limit. It also ruled that there was a power surge in the area that particular day that might have caused the problem. This exoneration meant that Ramnik's insurance claim stood an excellent chance of being cleared.

The meeting with Rowling turned out to be a minor bonanza for Ramnik and his business owner friends because she had come authorized to reduce their monthly premium and offer some extra benefits. He handed a copy of the fire department's report to her personally, paving the way for his claim to be settled. Two weeks later, he had received a check for $100,000.

The dramatic turnaround in his situation engendered great family happiness and prompted one more gathering to celebrate. Parthiv and Bela became even closer than before but kept up their mutual promise to wait before taking their relationship to the next level. They had not gone beyond kissing. Parthiv would joke that in keeping with the advice in the Sansthan book he was observing "partial celibacy and partial restraint."

He had started college during the day and working at the store in the evening. Ramnik familiarized him with store accounting and inventory management, which was still done very much in the old- fashioned, manual way. He suggested to his father that they needed to computerize everything, including labeling, pricing and inventory ordering and management. Ramnik was happy to see his son taking a keen interest in the business.

By the time Parthiv turned 17, Ramnik and Dipti began to notice a subtle difference in his attitude. They would frequently find him reading Sansthan books. He had already read the one about celibacy twice and asked many questions of his parents. Of his volition, he displayed the black and white photo of Guruji in his room with the sign "Life is sacrifice. Sacrifice is life." below it.

The parents were happy that their son was discovering something to emulate in the Sansthan philosophy but they were quite unsure what was causing the shift. Bela still visited but her visits were few and far between. Dipti once overheard Bela complain to Parthiv that he was no longer what he used to be. "Are we breaking up?" she asked him.

"No Bela, I am also becoming interested in other things in life. How can I break up with you? Even if I do, I will come running back to you," he said.

Parthiv's was feeling increasingly torn between his growing physical attraction for Bela and what he was reading in the Sansthan literature. In a particular passage in a chapter titled "Urges and Vitality" in the book about celibacy, Guruji had written: "Physical urges of sex are an enemy of the human body's vitality. The pleasure of sex may be good but it is short-lived and always extracts vitality in the form of semen. Yogis of India preserve that vitality by practicing celibacy. Their unspent semen becomes an eternal reservoir of vitality."

Parthiv found that after he read that particular passage his interactions with Bela began to feel strained. He particularly remembered how he turned away one evening when she was about to kiss his cheek. Bela was furious and she asked again, "Are you sure we are not breaking up? You are being weird with me. Why did you turn away?"

Realizing that he had messed up Parthiv thought it was perhaps the best time to explain to her what was going on.

"You know Bells, (That's what he called her when he was particularly vulnerable) I have been reading this book by Guruji. You know about it. I have told you that. I am scared but some of what he says has begun to appeal to me," Parthiv said. He fetched the copy of the book from his bedroom with the dog-eared page where the passage was. He read it out aloud. "Eew!" she said when she heard "unspent semen", and said, "Who is this guy?"

"It is Guruji. He lived for 92 years. How do you think he did that?" Parthiv said.

"I don't know. May be he was lucky. Are you saying he lived that long because he did not you know what?" Bela asked.

"It is possible. Why not?" Parthiv said.

"So what are you saying? Are you saying you want to be like him?" Bela asked. "I am not saying that but I am curious," he said

"You are thinking about it. Aren't you?" Bela persisted, her voice going up.

Parthiv cupped her face as if to calm her and said, "Bells, if I cannot discuss my feelings openly with you, with whom can I? Yes, I am thinking about it because I find it strange."

Bela was incensed enough to get up and stormed out of the house. She called her mother to pick her up. Parthiv went behind her and waited along as Bela's mother came half an hour later. In those 30 minutes, the two did not exchange a word. She left without so much as saying bye.

Three weeks after that one spring evening Parthiv surprised Ramnik and Dipti. "Dad, can we visit the ashram? I am keen to meet Swamiji," he said.

Unable to decide how to respond, Ramnik merely looked at him intently and then ran his fingers through his hair. Dipti hugged him. Finally, Ramnik asked, "Are you sure son?"

"Yes, dad. I want to see what the big deal is," he said. "See how? You mean just visit?" Dipti asked.

"Yes but also see if I want to join," Parthiv said.

Both Ramnik and Dipti had to sit down on hearing this. Dipti eyes welled up. She started crying. Ramnik too could not fight back his tears.

"Why are you two crying, mom, dad?" Parthiv said.

"Nothing beta, we are just overcome with emotions. It is so sudden. Has something happened?" Dipti asked.

"I have been thinking ever since the fire and how things have turned around, especially with the insurance. As dad said after the fire, there is a signal here," Parthiv said.

Ramnik cupped Parthiv's face and sobbed uncontrollably. After regaining some composure he said, "I don't know how I feel about this. I am not sure."

Dipti said, "I don't want to lose you. You are the only child we have."

"But dad I have heard you say how you regret not becoming a monk," Parthiv said. "Yes but if I had we would not be having this conversation," Ramnik said.

The three went quiet as they all sat together in the sofa, Parthiv's head resting in Dipti's lap and feet in Ramnik's. A while later, all three had fallen asleep.

CHAPTER 11

Bela considered Jay a friend but not so good as to share her confidences. Also, she was rather chary of his radical views about traditions. At 18, he was the only legal adult among the immediate circle of her friends and cousins. In most situations, Jayendra's worldview, such as it was, was compelling for his friends simply because it was so contrary to what they heard their parents tell them at home.

Bela was not particularly fond of his language, which others found entertaining simply because it was forbidden for them and they would never use it. Profanity was Jay's default language. Despite the misgivings, she decided to talk to him about Parthiv's changing personality.

Jay picked her up a couple of days after Bela had left Parthiv's house in a huff. They met at an Indian fast food place called "Fataafat Chataachat", Jay's favorite hangout. The three of them frequented the place and no one would think it odd to see them together without Parthiv. They ordered a bunch of snacks.

"'Tsup Bela? What's bugging you? Is Parth messing with you," Jayendra, always the straight shooter said.

"No Jay. You know him. He is generally so cool," she said.

"Then what are we discussing here?" Jay said and took an extended sip from his cheekoo milkshake.

"Something has got into his head. He is reading the Sansthan books all the time. He is really into some shit about celibacy. He read me a stupid passage from it about unspent semen and said how one should preserve it," Bela said.

Jay burst out laughing, letting out a spray of the milkshake. Luckily, it did not smear Bela. "Unspent what? Whatthefuck? He read you that?" Jay said and laughed again.

"This is not funny, Jay. You are such a jerk. I think he is breaking up with me," Bela said. "Only an asshole would break up with you," Jay said.

"No Jay, I think he is going to," Bela said.

Jay suddenly became thoughtful and said after a few seconds. "You know my dad is behind all this. He brings those dickheads from Bear Valley and forces young boys to join the shit there. He is forcing me to become a monk and then never have sex ever again. He does not know me. I am going to get laid so much before that," Jay said.

Bela was so exasperated that Jay had made it about himself and disregarded her problem altogether that she shouted, "Whatthefuck, Jay?" Other customers briefly looked at her and then she apologized to them. Fortunately for her, they were all non-Indian and did not care beyond a point.

"I am sorry, Bela. I am also getting frustrated at the shit that happens at home with my dad. If you think Parthiv is down with that shit, then we need to talk to him," he said. "Let's go get him."

Bela was incredulous at Jay's suggestion. However, as she thought about it, she thought it might be a good idea for the three of them to talk it over. She said, "Yeah, you call him."

Jay called Parth and said, "Hey monk-boy, have you jerked off yet?"

Bela was embarrassed but could not do anything. She could hear Parthiv laughing. That relieved her.

"Listen Bela and I are coming to pick you up. Get ready. We will eat out tonight. My treat," Jay said.

Bela could sense that Parthiv had gone quiet. Jay solved it for her saying, "Dude, just get ready. Will be there in 15."

Half an hour later, all three were back at the restaurant. Bela and Parthiv sat together with Jay sitting opposite. Bela, who was wearing a micro mini, made it a point to sit very close to Parthiv. She grabbed his hand put it on her thigh. He coiled back but did not say anything. She did it again. He withdrew it again.

Jay could sense that something mischievous was going on under the table. "You guys want me to get you a room? I know a decent motel on El Camino," he said.

Parthiv, trying hard to contain his anger, said, "Listen Bells, You are hot. I get it. I want it too but I also want to understand the other side."

"What other side? The side where you keep it down?" Jay said making a gesture of masturbation.

"What is with you two anyway? Bells, you left pissed off that day and never called. Now you bring me here with Jay to do God knows what. I told you I am going through something that I need to sort out myself. I love you and can never break up with you," Parthiv said.

Jay started to clap, saying, "Wow! That was intense. Did you hear that, Bela? He loves you. But does not want to be with you. What a dick!"

Bela decided that time was right for her to confront Parthiv.

"I want to know if you are staying with me or joining the monks. Have you seen the way some of them look at women?" she asked.

"I cannot tell you now. I have told dad to take me to Bear Valley. I want to see for myself," Parthiv said.

"See what, man? They just stop you from enjoying life," Jay said. "I still want to see," Parthiv said.

Bela got up and said to Jay, "I want you to drop me home. You come back for this jerk."

Jay, who also had the knack of diffusing tension, said, "Let's do this. Fuck all this for now. Let's just have great snacks. Let's not talk about it now. Who knows Parthiv may wake up and find some sense."

The trio agreed and ordered more snacks. They sat there for another hour or so and talked about everything except the Sansthan. Finally, as they got up to leave, Parthiv said, "I will never forget this evening. Bells, I love you so much but I have to do this."

Bela decided not to say anything. Jay said, "If you go, I go too. Let's change those dickheads."

CHAPTER 12

Parthiv's decision to go to Bear Valley and potentially join it threw family equations out of gear in ways none of them had anticipated. Although both Ramnik and Dipti had considered the possibility, they had believed all along that it would be they who would have to convince their son. They were not prepared for Parthiv preempting them.

A 17-year-old deciding to seriously consider leading a life of a celibate may have held some appeal as a television show or even a movie but for Ramnik and Dipti the idea of losing their only child to an ashram had gradually begun to shake up their emotional foundation.

The insurance claim coming through meant that Ramnik was no longer worried about his financial future even though he still needed to focus on growing the store's inventory again and expand business. In his spare moments at the store as he sat inside his cabin alone, he would start panicking about the day when Parthiv actually decided to leave.

It was a strange turn of events because he had at least theoretically considered sending Parthiv to Bear Valley to become a monk. He thought he would be able to deal with his son's absence because it was in aid of what he thought was a great cause. He did not anticipate the kind of wrenching that had begun to set in in his heart. What compounded this feeling for him was that Parthiv betrayed no nerves. He went about his routine such as going to school and occasionally dropping by at the store rather normally. Since his school graduation, he had become much firmer in his resolves.

Whatever he did, he did with unusual clarity. It was as if in one year he had grown up ten.

Dipti, who spent more time with Parthiv, noticed that after reading the Sansthan books he had become quietly assertive and confident. It was as if he had discovered his calling in reading the Siddhi philosophy. Unlike Ramnik, Dipti felt guilty at having exposed him to such ideas so early in his life. The Sansthan books in the Patel home, which rarely got picked up earlier, were extensively dog-eared now. Parthiv no longer watched television. He was on the net often but that did not seem to be for the kind of fun that a teenager would seek. The Sansthan site was his home page now.

A time came when Dipti seriously began to worry about the direction that Parthiv was taking. One weekday when she was alone, she called Ela Sheth, Ramnik's first cousin. She thought Parthiv needed a counterview from someone who was born here, shared the idiom and whom Parthiv respected.

"Ela, I need to meet you. Do you have any time this week?" Dipti said.

"Diptiben, it is great to hear from you. You don't have to ask me for time. When would you like to meet?" Ela said from her opulent office in Los Altos.

"The sooner the better. I want to talk to you about Parth," Dipti said. "Parth? Is he okay? What's wrong?" Ela said, sounding worried.

"Oh no no, nothing like that but I will tell you when we meet," Dipti said.

"I have some time this afternoon between meetings. Why don't I pick you up in another half an hour?" Ela said.

"Really? Can we meet right away? I thought you would have no time," Dipti said. "It's family, Diptiben. Everything else can wait," Ela said. "See you soon."

Dipti had planned to go to a restaurant first but changed her mind and decided to speak to Ela in the comfort of her home. Ela was dressed in a dark rust business suit, light pink shirt with an orange scarf. Her hair was slicked back. She cut a picture of corporate formalness but looked fetching.

"My my, I have never seen you in this attire. You look…powerful," Dipti said. They both laughed at Dipti's description.

Dipti asked her, "Ela, have you had anything to eat? I have something I made last night. You might like it. It is sabudana khichdi."

"No Diptiben, I won't eat. I skip lunch, I had some salad during an earlier meeting," Ela said, "But I will have your famous masala tea."

Dipti made two cups and they settled down in the living room. "I need your advice and may be even your help," Dipti said. "Sure. Tell me what I can do," Ela said.

"Parthiv says he wants to join the Sansthan," Dipti said, knowing that bit of information was enough explain to Ela her terrible predicament.

"What are you saying? Are you sure?" Ela asked.

"Yes, in the past six months or so Parth has changed a lot. He is both more confident than before and talks mostly about the Sansthan and its philosophy," Dipti said.

"How did that happen? Has Ramnikbhai been pushing Parth?" Dipti said.

"No. It is Parth who is pushing us. That is what I mean. Things have turned around completely. We are on the defensive now and we don't know what to do. Even Ramnik, who would normally be pleased with his son taking any interest in the Sansthan, is worried now," Dipti said.

"Do you want me to talk to Parth?" Ela said.

"That is the reason I wanted to talk to you. I think you should take him out or call him to your place before it is too late," Dipti said and became emotional.

"Of course, Diptiben. It is my duty. You know what I think about the Sansthan and Raghu Vishwa," Ela said, "I would be more than happy to talk some sense into his head. He is still a teenage boy. I am sure it is that rebellious phase. Do you remember how I nearly did that movie 'Unfinished Love'? Mercifully, the director rejected me because I was too wooden."

Dipti and Ela spoke for about an hour before the latter had to leave for a board meeting of her company. Ela, never the one to hold back opinions, said as a parting comment, "I have been telling Ramnikbhai for years that the Sansthan is a racket. They prey upon Indian families here in America who are so desperate to cling on to their culture. You should have thrown away all those books a long time ago."

Dipti reflexively defended the Sansthan even though she agreed with the gist of what Ela had said. "You can certainly learn some good values from them but you don't have to become a lifelong monk for that."

Just as Ela was leaving, Parth came home with Jay. The two boys greeted Ela with great enthusiasm with Jay throwing in, "Elaben you look hot."

Parth, curious to find out why Ela was visiting on a working day, said, "Everything okay, Elafai?" She said it was. Before getting into her Basalt Black Metallic Porsche 918 Spyder, she told Parth, "I am planning to invite you this weekend for a spin. Be ready." Parthiv just smiled while Jay, ever the flirt, said, "Hey, I am standing right here. And I am not even your nephew."

Ela said, "You, some other time. This time it is between Parth and I" and whizzed away.

CHAPTER 13

The topic of Parth's inclination to join the Sansthan did not come up through the week as Ramnik was busy restoring the store's inventory back to its pre-fire levels and upgrading its look a bit to increase business. He wanted to create a tiny tea and snacks lounge with more contemporary furniture at the right hand side of the main entrance. His banker had referred a young interior designer to him.

The designer, Stella paid a couple of visits that week to take the measurement and come up with a few design ideas. Ramnik remembered what Ela had once told him: "I know yours is an Indian grocery store but must it look like one?" She had said that there were many young tech workers coming to El Camino Real who might get attracted to a trendy looking tea lounge. It was that idea which had set him off on getting Stella.

Dipti had not told Ramnik about her meeting with Ela and how she had requested her to lean on Parth to change his mind. Although Ramnik had a great fondness for his cousin, he was uncomfortable with her views about the Sansthan. Her high lifestyle and bohemian ways did not sit well with him. He was afraid that Parth and others might emulate her. However, he also knew that almost no one else in his immediate family had nearly the wealth to live it up the way Ela did. He knew Bela's parents were equally wealthy but were circumspect in their spending. Bela's mother Meena had once joked "Bela was like Ela with a B in her."

Bela looked up to Ela for all the reasons which Ramnik found unacceptable. She was single at 32 and had the reputation to have many liaisons. At one point, the Patel clan was agog with the rumor that Ela was dating three men, two white and one Hispanic with one at least 20 years her senior. To Ramnik's dismay, she had confirmed the rumor. "Ramnikbhai, each knows about the other two. I like an open lifestyle. It is more natural than celibacy that all of you are so enamored of," she had said.

Somewhere along the line, both Ramnik and Dipti admired Ela's independence but could never practice her ways themselves.

That Saturday morning, Ela dropped by at the Patels' to Ramnik's pleasant surprise. "Ela, you never drop by like that. To what do we owe this great surprise?" Ramnik asked. Since Dipti had told her not to mention their little chat, Ela said, "I had been meaning to take Parth for a spin in my new Porsche. So here I am. I will drop him back in the evening. We might go up to the Big Sur and back."

Intrigued but happy Ramnik said, "Why not? The boy needs to go out. These days he reads the Sansthan books all the time."

Parthiv came down and hugged Ela. "Elafai, I am excited to ride with you." The two left soon afterward.

The aunt and nephew drove for about three hours and reached the Big Sur in time for lunch. Ela had a favorite bakery that she visited often. It was a laidback place and offered a host of food, her favorite being their wood-fired cheese pizza with the toppings such as fresh jalapenos, olives, tomatoes, onions and zucchini.

"So Parth, what have you been up to? What are the plans after graduation? You are doing accountancy, I believe," Ela said.

"Yes, I am. After the fire I was a bit distracted but since then I have had time to read quite a bit," he said without venturing to tell her what it was that he was reading.

"What kind of books are you reading? Game of Thrones? That's fun," Ela said, trying to hide the fact that she already knew from Dipti that he was mostly into Sansthan literature.

"No Elafai, I have been reading only Sansthan books. The one about celibacy is very interesting. It requires so much confidence—celibacy I mean. The book says it strengthens one's body," he said.

Ela, trying not to show her disapproval immediately, "That's nice Parth but you should consider fun reading too. Those Sansthan books can always be read later. It is fun age for you now," Ela said.

"I know but I am very interested in what they have to say. I don't know if mom told you or not but I am going to visit Bear Valley with dad. I am keen to join," he said with a matter-of-fact tone that unsettled Ela.

It was a delicate moment and Ela did not want to complicate it by giving him her familiar derisive rejection of the Sansthan. She could sense that Parthiv had made up his mind as much as what Dipti had told her. Hearing from him directly had a different effect. Ela had seen him grow up. She was at the hospital when he was born. In fact, Ela had given the name Parthiv. To see that cheerful but quiet nephew grow up into a young man talking the virtues of celibacy with her was a strange feeling. They had never discussed anything so personal. She could see that Parthiv felt more comfortable talking to his young and "cool" aunt about it than he might have with anyone else, including and particularly his parents.

"So let me ask you this. What happens to Bela?" Ela asked.

"Bela understands that it is over between her and I. I love her still but I have to see what a monk's life means," Parthiv said.

"Does she understand it or you gave her no choice? She still does not understand everything about this subject just as you don't even if you pretend," Ela said.

Before Parthiv could respond, Ela continued, "You know what a celibate monk's life is? It is a very tough life. It is also a very boring and disciplined life. All that you think as fun will go away. This ride we took today that you liked so much? Over. Friends? Over. Meeting parents? Rarely. I guarantee you will hate the next day."

Parthiv thought about it for a few moments and said, "I know it is not going to be easy but I want to try it. It's kind of cool that people fall at monks' feet. They look so calm."

Ela was beginning to get exasperated but maintained her composure. "Listen Parth, I cannot stop you if you are bent on doing it but I think it is a stupid idea because you have read a couple of books. I don't want you to regret your decision. Once you go in, there is no turning back," she said.

"Why can't I leave if I don't like it there?" Parthiv said.

"Honey, it does not work that way. They wouldn't let you walk out because one fine day you lost interest. You are there for life," Ela said sensing a slight doubt creeping into his resolve.

"I don't want to walk out. I want to first see what it is about. That is why I have asked dad to take me there soon," he said.

The two talked for another hour about the implications of Parthiv's decision. She also pointed out that him still not being legally adult, his parents could compel him to follow their instructions. It was not his decision to take until he turned 18 but even after that his parents could always play a role.

"I will turn 18 in four months' time, Elafai. I can wait for four months. Then I can decide on my own," Parthiv said throwing Ela off a bit.

"Sure you can but I want you to very carefully think through this. I know how the Sansthan works, how crazy its people are when it comes to their interests. I have spoken to many of their followers although the monks never speak to women," she said. She told him about the fundraiser where she had had a very public showdown with Raghu Vishwa who was caught unawares by her presence. Being one of the two founders, her company's CEO and co-founder Jignesh Vakharia had no choice but to invite her. Enough care was taken to ensure that Raghu Vishwa and Ela did not sit face-to-face. Despite that, Ela had managed to corner him.

Ela and Parthiv left the Big Sur around 5 p.m. and reached home 8 p.m. On the way back, she had tried one more time to put things in perspective for him. "Do you know ordinary monks sleep in one large hall? There is no privacy. There will be no privacy for the rest of your life. You will be told everyday what to do and what not to do. You will not get to watch TV or play video games. There will be no cell phones. Think about all that Parth. It sounds easy but if you to live like that forever you will find it impossible," she said.

After reaching home Dipti and Ramnik invited her to have dinner. She was not so keen but could not say no. Dipti had told Ramnik about the purpose of the aunt-nephew's dayout. Parthiv retired to his room after a quick meal while the three adults chatted a bit.

"I have tried my best today. I think nothing can dissuade him. He is determined to give it a shot because he thinks if he does not like it, he can quit. I explained to him it does not work that way. But he is not going to change his mind. I even pulled the legal age argument but he said he would wait until he turns 18 in four months. The visit to Bear Valley that he wants to go on is a sort of a dry run for him. I don't know what else to do other than really scaring him," Ela said.

Both Ramnik and Dipti looked troubled but did not say anything. Ela finally said, "It is getting late. I think I should go. Let's talk again soon. I know this is worrisome for you but we cannot let a child decide something so momentous." She got into her Porsche. Before driving, she texted one of her boyfriends, saying, "I have been a celibate for three days. Let's end that."

CHAPTER 14

Dipti kept waking up throughout that Friday night, Saturday morning. Several times, she peeped through Parth's bedroom that was ajar, as if making sure that he was still there. A couple of times she caressed Parth's forehead, careful not to wake him up. Father and son had planned to visit Bear Valley on Saturday. She knew she was running out of ways to stop him from leaving. Finally, she decided she could no longer stay in bed and came down to the kitchen at 5.30 a.m.

Mauve sunlight had begun to smudge the inky darkness. It promised to be a brilliant California day but Dipti saw no promise in it for herself. She was reminded of an expression in Gujarati she frequently heard from her mother. "Pet ma faal pade chhey" (There is a strange vacuum in the stomach), her mother would say sometimes when she had that sinking feeling. Dipti had the feeling that morning. She made a cup of tea but burst out crying before she could take the first sip.

Ramnik got up around 6.45, looking well rested. "You look so exhausted, Dipti. I heard some movements last night. Are you okay?" he asked.

Dipti looked up and revealed her bloodshot red eyes. Ramnik was shocked and said, "Have you been crying?" In a rare show of affection, he hugged her, gently massaging her head. She kept crying. "Why are you crying, Dipti? Parth is coming back with me. He cannot decide this on his own. We are still alive," he said firmly.

Dipti just could not stop sobbing. "What if he stays on today?" she said barely managing to form the question in the midst of her sobs.

"I am not going to let him. He is not going to do it. He promised me that," Ramnik said even as he sounded that he did not believe his own words.

"I am going to talk to him before you leave," Dipti said.

For the next hour or so, the Patels were silent, going about their chores with a measure of disengagement that comes from nervousness. Ramnik tried to read the San Jose Mercury News but could not focus. He folded it and dropped it on the floor. He stepped out into their small front garden and turned on the sprinklers. A spray from one of them wetted the edge of his pajama and bare toes. The soothing coolness of the water seemed to help his nerves. He went back inside after 15 minutes to find Parth eating his breakfast. "Morning, Dikra," he said with a cheerfulness that was disproportionate to what he was feeling.

"Hi, dad," Parth replied. "What time are we leaving?" he asked without a trace of any discernible emotion. His matter of fact tone at this age was unsettling for both Ramnik and Dipti. Dipti saw an opportunity in that question and jumped in before Ramnik could answer.

"Parth, why are you doing this?" she said.

"Mom, because…" he said still betraying his teenage by leaving the sentence unfinished after "because".

"Parth, because is not an answer. I want to know why you are doing this. I can stop you, you know," Dipti said.

"I am doing this because I want to understand that life. You can stop me for the next four months but not after that," Parth said. The firmness of his resolve and tone surprised even him.

Dipti looked at him with a mixture of anger and resignation and walked off. He knew when she did that she was truly upset. That always brought out the child in him. He ran after her as she went upstairs. "Mom, don't be angry. I love you," Parth said but Dipti kept walking.

"What is the point of loving me if you are not going to be around to love me?" Dipti said. That stumped Parth. He did not know what to say.

"I will try and forget you gradually. May be someday I will," Dipti continued. She cried again.

Parth stood in the doorway to her bedroom, looking lost. Downstairs, Ramnik held his head in his hands and kept mumbling, "What is going on, God? Is this your idea of family and life?"

Unable to process the sudden change in his parents' mood, Parth went back to his room and shut the door. He stood in front of the portrait of Guruji, looked at it intently for a few seconds and started reciting the Gayatri Mantra "Om bhur bhuva swaha…" Unlike the previous years when he used to say it in mock seriousness and maul the pronunciation, this time he sounded clearly better. He had been practicing it.

Half an hour later, Parth and Ramnik were on their way to Bear Valley. Dipti did not even come out of her bedroom to say bye to him. He shouted before leaving, "Mom, I will see you tomorrow."

The two-hour drive to the Sansthan was largely uneventful since Parth fell asleep. Ramnik played some Hindi movie songs from his favorite collection 'The Grand Golden 1950s', which consisted of mostly Mohammad Rafi and Mukesh songs. In particular, he liked 'Brindavan ka Krishna Kanhaiya" from the 1957 movie 'Miss Mary'. If Parth heard anything other than the Gayatri Mantra out of his father's mouth, it was this song. The song never failed to move Ramnik. As he played it several times on the drive, he choked up.

The very real possibility that he might lose his son to the Sansthan was dawning on him as he entered the main gate shaped like two giant elephants locking their trunks 30 feet above the ground. The money to sculpt and transport that special gate from India was donated by the Indian community of the Bay Area. Ramnik had donated $501 towards the total budget of $25,000. There were 500 names of donors on a special pillar erected next to the gate. Ramnik was in the last column, being among the smallest donors. It read Ramnik/Dipti/Parthiv Patel.

Dhiru was waiting under the main canopy leading to main hall of the ashram to receive Ramnik and Parthiv. Parthiv woke up rubbing his eyes and said, "Oh, we are here? I fell asleep, dad."

Dhiru said Namaste to Ramnik even as Parth touched the former's feet, utterly surprising him. "Welcome to the Sansthan," Dhiru said, "You are just in time for lunch. Swamiji normally eats alone but today he has made an exception. He has expressed the wish to eat with you."

Ramnik smiled and said, "Ahobhagya (Our good fortune). Parth, let us wash up before we go in."

The meal was simple. Parth barely ate because it was not the kind he liked. Ramnik noticed that and made a mental note to the list of things he would tell him to discourage him. In keeping with the rules of the ashram, Raghu Vishwa did not talk during the meal. He did smile occasionally at Parth though. When Parth tried to ask a question, Dhiru shook his head to say not to talk. That added one more arrow to Ramnik's quiver. The meal was turning out to be an interesting learning lesson for Parthiv, giving him his first glimpse into his would-be life. At the end of the meal, Raghu Vishwa said a prayer and got up saying "Hari Om'.

The visitors were taken to Swamiji's austere office room where the silence was finally broken.

"So Parthiv, welcome to the Sansthan. I am pleasantly surprised to have you here. When Ramnikbhai mentioned some days ago that you wanted to visit, I was not sure if you would come. You are here now. Let us make the best of your stay. I believe you are going back tomorrow," Raghu Vishwa said.

"Yes, Swamiji. I am here because I am curious. I have read all Sansthan books at home many times," Parth said.

"Curiosity is the first step towards knowledge. So it is good. I have requested Dhirubhai to take you around along with your father. Spend as much time as you want and if you have any questions after that, ask me," Raghu Vishwa said.

Dhiru, Ramnik and Parth took their leave and began the tour of the facility. The first stop was a cavernous prayer hall. A giant lotus was hung upside down as a chandelier with its stem acting as the tether to the ceiling. If it were a circle, it would have a circumference of 200 feet. It was an impressive artifact aimed to make an immediate impact on visitors. Monks resident there were too accustomed to it to notice it any more. Looking at that Parth let out a whistle. The lotus had a gradient of pink with the light towards the tip of the petals and deeper pink in the middle. The lotus's stigma acted as a cluster of high wattage bulbs. On the floor underneath the lotus chandelier sat a carpet that precisely matched the contours of the flower above. It was a pink and yellow carpet.

Dhiru explained to Parthiv the importance of the lotus flower to Hindu culture and how the Sansthan has incorporated it in their iconography. He told him that the resident monks recited their hour-long prayer, engaged in an hour-long Yoga routine and an hour-long scriptural studies in the hall every day. "Those three hours are sacrosanct. The routine starts at 5.30 in the morning and ends 8.30. That's when monks break for a light breakfast," Dhiru said.

"Three hours every day?" Parth asked somewhat incredulously. "Why every day?"

Dhiru laughed and said, "Because prayers, rituals and studies are known as nitkram or things that happen on a regular basis. That is our culture."

Dhiru also recited some of the prayers and shlokas as well as demonstrated some of the Yoga asanas. "Swamiji has done this for nearly 60 years every day even though he has so much else to do," Dhiru said with unconcealed pride. "I have done it for 35 years."

From the prayer hall, the father and son were taken to the ashram canteen, which had four neatly laid rows tables, and chair that could seat 300 people. "What kind of breakfast is served here?" Parth asked.

"It is a light breakfast which is a mixture of Gujarati and South Indian items. Do you know what Idlis are?" Dhiru said.

"I have eaten those, yes," Parth said.

"We occasionally serve those. Some days it is batata pauha. We serve only two or three types but mainly it is these two. There is no tea or coffee allowed in the ashram," Dhiru said.

"So what do you drink with it? No juice?" Parthiv said.

"No juices or soda at all. Water and milk are allowed," Dhiru said.

Ramnik was beginning to enjoy the fact that Parthiv was getting gradually introduced to the rigors of the ashram life. He appeared to be keenly observing everything. He asked minute questions like a student joining a university. The trio then went to the residential wing of the ashram. It was a bit of a misnomer to call it a residential wing because essentially it was one huge hall with rows and rows of meticulously made-up beds under one roof. The beds were basic with two pillows and one blanket. Each had a small side unit on the right hand side for very small storage. The mouth of the pillowcases all faced one direction. The linen was ivory colored. Each bed had by its right hand side on the floor a red mat. The main isle, on whose two sides were the beds, was under a long carpet.

On a closer examination, Parth noticed that each side unit had one steel plate, one spoon, two bowls and one cup. They also had a tiny napkin each. There were individual lamps by the side. "No Lights After 9 P.M." said a sign posted at several places.

In the smaller wing adjacent to the sleeping hall were bathrooms and toilets. There were 50 of each. They looked as if they had never been used. They were that meticulously cleaned. There was no smell at all. The sign there said "No Bath Longer than 3 Minutes" Before Parthiv could calculate, Dhiru said, "There are 200 monks. Each takes about five minutes on ablutions etc. For now, it is four monks to a bathroom and toilet for five minutes each. You do the calculation. They have to wake up by 4 a.m."

"4 a.m.?" Parth asked again sounding a bit alarmed. Ramnik took a mental note again.

"Yes but you get used to it. That is why you must go to sleep at 9 p.m." Dhiru said. "That gives you seven hours of sleep."

The rest of the ashram tour was spent of telling Parth the kind of physical work the monks have to do in the upkeep of this large facility in terms of cleaning all the rooms, gardening, doing the dishes, chopping vegetables and washing all clothes and linen. Novitiates also had the added task of carrying out odd, random chores assigned by their seniors, which could also include massaging elderly monks' feet. In short, the monks were given next to no leisure time.

"So when do they get a break?" Parth asked.

"We allow five hours of recreation every other Sunday when the monks can play sports or watch educational TV. We show wholesome movies every two months. We show them documentaries as well," Dhiru said.

By the time the tour was over, it was about 6.30 in the evening, Swamiji's supper time. He had made an exception today to eat with the visitors both times. The supper was almost exactly the same as the lunch. Parthiv picked at his food. It was eaten without a word being exchanged.

Before retiring for the night, Raghu Vishwa asked the father and son to join them for a stroll. "What did you think of the visit, Parthiv?" he asked.

"It was interesting. I think it is a tough life but could be interesting," Parth said.

"I am told by Dhirubhai that you have read Guruji's book about celibacy many times," Raghu Vishwa said.

"Yes, Swamiji. I have almost memorized it," Parth said. Before Raghu Vishwa could respond to it, Parthiv said: "Physical urges of sex are an enemy of the human body's vitality. The pleasure of sex may be good but it is short-lived and always extracts vitality in the form of semen. Yogis of India preserve that vitality by practicing celibacy. Their unspent semen becomes an eternal reservoir of vitality."

"Wah, wah, I am very pleased. I am very pleased indeed. I don't think any monk here can say it as clearly as you just did. Ramnikbhai, you must be proud of your son," Raghu Vishwa said.

Ramnik feebly said, "Yes" sounding worried that the tour of the ashram had not had much effect on Parthiv.

"So, are you going to join us?" Raghu Vishwa asked. Ramnik was taken aback by the directness of the question. "We have not decided yet but today's visit will…"before Ramnik could complete the sentence, Parthiv interrupted and said, "When I turn 18 in four months, I will be here the day after my birthday."

Ramnik had to sit down on one of the stone benches. Dhiru, who was walking some steps behind the three, rushed to Ramnik and said, "May I get you some water? Ramnikbhai, there is nothing to worry. Parthiv is an exceptional child."

Raghu Vishwa patted Ramnik on the back and said, "He will be what you wanted to be but couldn't be."

CHAPTER 15

"**I** think we have lost him."

Those six words in Ramnik's text to Dipti before leaving Bear Valley dealt a staggering blow to her. For a few moments, she felt dizzy and disoriented. She had half a mind to call and yell at him but she realized it would serve no purpose and it would only make it worse.

She drank some water and decided to sit on a patio chair outside the main door. She knew it would take about two hours for them to reach. She was determined to sit there that long.

Ramnik and Parthiv were home by 5 p.m. that Sunday. Parthiv noticed Dipti sitting there, waiting and looking askance. He knew that look. It meant she was particularly incensed. Parth pretended not to notice and greeted her normally, "Hi mom, we are back." He hugged her but found no response. Standing behind him Ramnik signaled Dipti not to make a fuss. The three went in.

"Are you going to leave me?" Dipti asked straight as Parth removed his shoes.

He did not answer. She asked again. He did not answer. Dipti stood in the kitchen leaning on the island and holding her head in her palms. Parthiv was going through the fridge and grabbing random snacks saying, "I am so hungry."

Ramnik saw an opening for him to get in. "You know why you are so hungry, right? The ashram does not have the kind of food you like and what they have, is served only at specific times. You can't go snacking there like you do at home."

Parthiv was too busy eating to respond. After a few hungry bites, he finally said, "That doesn't matter, dad. I know this is going to be very tough but I have decided to go after I turn 18. I want to see it for myself."

Dipti picked up a pan and banged it on the island. She said, "Go right now if you want. I am no longer going to tell you anything. Do what you want with your life. Who am I to stop you?"

Both Ramnik and Parthiv were taken aback by Dipti's outburst. It had been building up since Saturday morning when Parthiv went to Bear Valley against her wish. It was compounded by her helplessness to convince a 17-year-old and her only child to boot. She continued to rant, "Doesn't the Sansthan teach you to respect your parents? Is it not part of Hindu culture? Where does it say in our scriptures that a son must defy his parents at any cost? I am telling you that if you join the Sansthan, you are dead to me."

She stormed out of the house and went for a walk with no shoes on. It was a behavior that was deeply unsettling for both father and son. Parthiv ran after her but Ramnik stopped him saying, "Don't. I think she needs to sort it out herself. You will only make it worse. I dislike what you are planning to do as much but I think I have no choice once you are 18. For the next four months, you are still under our control. Don't forget that."

"Dad, I don't get this. Ever since I was a child, both you and mom kept talking about our culture and how great it is. You always thrust Sansthan books and mantras in my face. You kept saying I must be a "Dahya dikra" and respect our traditions. Now that I am doing exactly that, you are both so upset. I just don't get this dad, I don't," he said in a tone of utter exasperation and went back to his room.

Ramnik went to his and decided to lay down for a bit. Dipti returned home after an hour or so looking chastened. She came up to the room and told Ramnik, "I don't feel like making any food. There is some leftover from the morning and some frozen food. Manage with that. I am not hungry. I am going to sleep early."

Ramnik was silent. He went down to switch on the television. The channel was set on the Hindi entertainment channel that carried "Teri Bindiya Mein Suraj Ki Lalima". It was a measure of Dipti's foul mood that she had either forgotten it was time for a new episode of the soap that night or deliberately chosen not to watch it in protest. It was a pity because Ramnik, not particularly inclined to watch anything, lingered on for a few minutes desultorily watching the unfolding drama. He could tell that the episode was building up towards a rapprochement that evening between the father-in-law and daughter-in-law. It was a high moment and a massive spoiler if he chose to reveal it to Dipti. He joked in his mind that spoiling it for her would be almost as upsetting as Parth leaving and laughed.

Parth did not come down to eat anything even though Ramnik called him for dinner. Ramnik ate some salad and bundi raita and retired for the night. Dipti was fast asleep and serenely so.

Monday morning came as a relief for Ramnik because he had the store to go to. Its mixture of fragrances was his getaway zone. He also had the work on the tea and snack lounge to look forward to. It had begun to take shape. Stella was already there supervising the carpenter and others. She was dressed in a YSL faux black wrap skirt and a crewneck T-shirt with pink polka dots. She looked stunning and somewhat distracting for Ramnik. It was one of those rare moments when Ramnik noticed an attractive woman purely because she was attractive. Stella greeted him effusively. She called him Ram but sounded like she was saying Rem. "So Rem, the lounge is coming along pretty good, don't you think? This is going to look very hip," she said.

Ramnik could make out the broad contours of the lounge and loved what he saw. "It might be out of sync with the rest of the store," he said.

"Let's do up the whole store," Stella said.

"Oh, I wish. Who am I going to do it for?" Ramnik said subconsciously projecting problems with Parth.

Unsuitable Celibate?

"Why do you say that? Parth would love to have a store like this," she said.

Ramnik got lost in thoughts. Stella noticed that and said, "Where have you disappeared, stranger?"

Although Stella did not at all mean to be excessively friendly, her manner could be misread by a middle-aged man to mean that. Had it not been for Ramnik's wistful reflection about the problems at home, he would have noticed the "stranger" part of her question.

"It's nothing. Just some stuff at home. Anyway, this is looking good. I don't know about the store. No budget for this for now," he said and went to his office.

Stella got busy with instructing his team.

That evening Dipti and Parth visited the store. Peace seemed to have been restored between them. Dipti suggested that they should go out for dinner. Ramnik liked the idea. Just as they were leaving Stella came back to check on how much her team had finished that day. She did not know Ramnik would still be there. She hugged Dipti and Parth. "It is so lovely to see you both. Did you guys see the lounge area?" she asked.

Dipti said she did and liked it very much. Parth said it looked "way cool." "If it is way cool, it is yours," Stella joked. "You can run this."

"Yeah, right," Parth said. He knew what he meant as did his parents but it was lost on Stella who just laughed.

It was not lost on Parth how good Stella looked. He felt some stirrings but quickly banished the thought. He also thought of Bela and the Sansthan and celibacy, all in a flash.

As they were leaving, Ramnik said impulsively, "Why don't we invite Stella to join?" To his surprise, both Dipti and Parth agreed immediately.

Stella saw that as an opportunity to possibly get the commission to redo for the entire store in the near future and agreed to join.

It turned out to be an amiable dinner at Mumbai Brasserie. A popular restaurant, the four met many common friends, including Jayendra who was there with a girl, whom he did not introduce. The presence of his date for the evening did not discourage him from flirting with Stella who played along a bit.

Stella and Parth spoke about various things, including and much to the discomfort of the parents, religion. Parth mentioned the Sansthan but skirted his decision to join. That was because he had agreed with Dipti not to talk about it until he turned 18. He kept his word and mentioned the Sansthan only fleetingly.

Dipti was surprisingly voluble with Stella whose enthusiasm seemed to have soothed the tension among the Patel family.

What began as a tense and unpleasant day had turned out to be refreshingly upbeat for them, thanks in large measure to Stella.

CHAPTER 16

The tea and snacks lounge at Ramnik's store was christened "Indian Tea & Snacks Lounge (It's Lounge)". Parth suggested the name and its trendy abbreviation. By some coincidence, it was complete just one week before Parth's 18th birthday. To mark the two occasions, the Patels decided to host a joint celebration at the lounge.

The lounge could accommodate 56 people. The celebration on the evening of its opening and Parth's birthday had a guest list of 50 who included Parth's best school friend George O'Keefe and, surprisingly, James the jock. Bela and family were very much there. So were Jayendra and family, Ela and family, all the cousins and Stella.

The store had been professionally cleaned and arranged for the evening. The lighting and signage were changed at Stella's instance. It made the store look rather high-end, unlike the other Indian grocery stores in the area. The guests noticed the transformation and commented on it favorably. Bela, in particular, was so taken in by the lounge, its hip, contemporary ambience and its name that she had tears in her eyes. "Thiv, this rocks," she told Parth and kissed on his cheek. Parthiv quickly clarified, "Bells, I did nothing. It is all Stella and dad." He introduced Stella to Bela and while the pleasantries were being exchanged between the two, Jayendra joined in with a joke, "Bela and Stella, What a lucky fella!" They all laughed.

The twin celebration turned out to be spectacularly joyous. The guests loved the food, especially the way Stella had displayed the whole spread.

In keeping with the new look of the store, Ramnik and Dipti were dressed in what many cousins thought were the "coolest" clothes they had ever worn. All that was courtesy of Stella who seemed to have pulled out all stops. She had brought in a couple of potential clients with Ramnik's permission for a commission.

Parth and Bela stuck together like never before. The two got into an animated conversation with George and James, reminiscing about the school days. Both the schoolmates, one a tormentor and the other a truce-maker, were very pleased with the lounge and the food. "This is some bad shit, Pee-Pee. I love this," James said. George, as sober as ever, said, "I am going to bring my girlfriend here."

"You have a girlfriend?" both Parth and James asked in unison and surprise.

"Why didn't you bring her with you?" Bela asked.

"Oh, I thought she was not part of the invitation," George said.

"Oh come on, George. This is an Indian party. The whole of Sunnyvale is part of the invitation. Call her now," Bela said.

After some hesitation, George called his girlfriend Stacy. James said he had recently broken up with his and was single. He had been eyeing Stella all evening. "How old is that one?" James asked pointing at Stella.

Parth said he was not sure but probably 25.

"She will do for me," James said and asked Parth to introduce him to her. James put on his best jock swagger and shook hands with her. Stella noticed his good looks and seemed to warm up to him.

"Pee Pee, I am going to ditch you now," James said as he walked away with Stella toward her two potential clients.

Bela went to be with her parents as George and Parth got talking.

"I need to tell you something, O'Keefe," Parth said. He always called him by his last name. "Tsup?" George asked.

"Let's sit down and talk a bit," Parth said.

"Oh, that serious?" George asked in mock wonder. "Could be," Parth said.

The two found a corner table and started talking. Bela noticed that but did not want interrupt two old friends. However, she could sense from their body language that Parth had probably told George of his intention to join the Sansthan. George's mouth was agape. He kept looking at other guests as if trying to find out if one else had been privy to what he had just heard. He got up a couple of times from his chair and gesticulated with his hand, like he was saying, "Really?"

"Who else knows about it?" George asked.

"My parents do. Bela does and Jay does. The rest will find out soon. I was waiting to turn 18 so that my mom and dad wouldn't be able to stop me," Parth said.

George let out a whistle and said again "Really? A monk? A monk like the one who does not get laid?"

It was for the first time that George had been so direct in his expression about sex. He came from a conservative Catholic family that followed most of the principles of Catholicism. Parth could not imagine that someone like him would actually use the words "get laid." That told him about the measure of George's incredulity.

George kept looking at Parth in disbelief and said, "Fuck, man. You mean no fucking? Ever?"

"Hey what's up with that O'Keefe? I have never heard you use the F word before. What changed?" Parth said.

"Nothing changed. You did. I can't believe this. Are you sure? What about Bela? Is she good with this?" George continued.

"I am sure and no, she is not good with it. But I have to do this," Parth said.

"How can she be good with this? You love her and she loves you. Don't you have to do something about that?" George said.

"This is bigger than us, O'Keefe," Parth said. "There is more I want to tell you." "There is more too? What more?" George said.

"I am going to announce it this evening," Parth said.

George ran out of the store. Bela saw that and kept rushing to Parth. "What happened? Did you two fight? Why did George run out?" she said.

"No, we did not fight," Parth said and went after George. So did Bela.

The three talked animatedly outside. Dipti, who was acutely conscious of what her son had said about his plans on turning 18, saw them. She sensed that it had to do with Parth's decision but decided not to get involved between the three childhood friends.

Outside, George and Bela argued with Parth feverishly, trying to persuade him not to spoil the evening by announcing his intentions. "Listen Parthiv, if you do that, you will never see me again," she said. Parthiv knew every time she addressed him by his full name she was deadly serious.

"You cannot ruin everything this evening. Look at your mom and dad. They are so happy. Don't fuck it up for them?" George said.

"Why are you so foul-tongued, O'Keefe?" Parth said. "Because I am pissed off by what you told me," George said.

After moments of silence, Parth said, holding Bela's hand, "Bells and O'Keefe, only because the two of you say so I will not announce it this evening. I will do it at the right time at home and only to mom and dad. They can tell the rest."

"But you are leaving for sure?" George said. "I am," Parth said.

Bela broke down.

George, finding the moment awkward, went back inside the store. Bela and Parth instinctively held hands.

"Let's make a deal," Bela said. "Tell me," Parth said.

"I turn 18 in six months. Let's make love once and I will let you go," Bella said.

Parth was taken aback by the proposition. He looked at her quizzically and then laughed. "Are you serious, Bells? I cannot do that," he said.

"Why can't you do that? You are not confused between being a celibate and a virgin, are you?" Bella challenged.

Parth thought long and hard. Before he could say anything, Bella continued, "That would be the real challenge. Let us see if you can practice celibacy after tasting sex once."

Bella, who was crying barely moments earlier, looked like a very different person. She sounded mischievous and aggressive.

"You know how many guys would kill to hit this?" she said tracing the contours of her body. "Three of them are right here—Jay, George and James. I just have to look at them funny and they will come running."

Parth could not believe what he was hearing. He also knew that what she was saying was true. He remembered that it was his relationship with Bela, regarded as among the hottest girls in school, that often won him reprieve from the jocks and bullies because they had a sneaking admiration for him because she was his girlfriend.

"Okay, that's a deal," Parthivs said. They stole a kiss and went inside.

James and Stella had hooked up and left together. The rest of the guests started leaving soon afterwards. By the time the party ended, it was 11 p.m. Only Bela's and Parthiv's families remained. They decided to go to Bela's house for coffee.

CHAPTER 17

For the next six months, Parthiv remained torn between celibacy and Bela's impending 18th birthday. The more he thought of celibacy, the more he also thought of sex. In particular, he thought of the deal the two had made on his 18th birthday.

Every time he thought of Bela saying, "You know how many guys would kill to hit this?" and tracing the contours of her body, he felt an uncontrollable urge to make love to her. In those moments he turned to 'Celibacy and Restraint: Ingredients of a Happy Life' but that barely helped. In the week before Bela's 18th birthday, he sexted her so frequently that she began to think she might just preempt his decision to become a monk.

Being the only child, Bela's parents decided to throw a big party for her birthday. It was a themed affair, with the theme being "She's Sexy and She Knows It." The theme selection was Bela's, as a teaser to the deal she had made with Parthiv. The day after the birthday was a Friday and Bela and Parthiv had decided to spend the weekend together in the Big Sur. Her father had booked a room for them at a high-end boutique hotel for three nights.

Under ordinary circumstances, Ramnik and Dipti would have bristled with moral indignation at any suggestion of Parth going away with Bela to a resort and spend night together. In fact, Mahendra and Meena's liberal ways generally and with their daughter particularly were a point of friction between the two families. Mahendra and Meena were considered radical among the circle of friends that the Patels maintained. It took the Patels a long time to get past Bela's dressing style and see her for the warm and caring friend that she had been to Parthiv.

With Parthiv's Sansthan decision looming large now, the Patels thought that whatever might transpire during their weekend together could potentially alter their son's plans. Dipti even told Ramnik, to his utter surprise, that she wished that the two would "go all the way."

"Once he discovers those pleasures, he might change his mind," Dipti told Ramnik. "You are being optimistic. I think you underestimate Parth's resolve," Ramnik said.

The birthday party was quite a glittering spectacle. Bela chose a black Soutache Sequin Floral Dress and red Evie Crystal heels. She looked stunning. When she walked down her mansion's elaborate staircase in an orchestrated entry whistles and woos went off. Parth looked utterly captivated. Having been with her for six years, he had developed a certain indifference towards her physical attractiveness. That evening he rediscovered her with a passion he did not think he harbored. For a few moments, he felt both jealous and insecure that her beauty was shared with others that evening. He then remembered their planned weekend and felt greatly aroused.

A mélange of feelings swirled around in Parthiv's mind as Bela walked up to him and gave a peck on his cheek. He remembered a passage from the Sansthan book that said, "Physical pleasures have been made so powerful and irresistible precisely to test your resolve. The more yearn for them, the more you should avoid them." But he also remembered the severely regimental atmosphere of the Sansthan during his visit to Bear Valley with his father. Monks looked and acted like automatons. Some of them looked visibly repressed. The idea of waking up at four every morning and getting sucked into an unwavering routine of scriptural training as opposed to waking up next to Bela was not at all comforting for him. However, for that evening and for the next three days he decided to banish the Sansthan from his mind.

The birthday celebrations entailed a band, a skit, a fashion show and a whole lot of dancing in Bela's massive backyard. It turned out to be a memorable event with all friends and cousins letting their hair down and making the most of the entertainment laid out by her family. For once, Parthiv too let go of his inhibitions and danced away. Bela was much sought after as a dance partner but she made sure that she was not torn away too long from Parthiv.

She had never seen him so happy and without any guards. The absence of restraint and brooding austerity made him look rather handsome that night. She even saw a couple of her friends flirting with him. And he did not seem to fight it. It was as if he was just beginning to discover the excitements of teenage. Both Dipti and Ramnik noticed that as well and smiled several times at each other. Swept up by the mood of the celebration they too danced. It was a rare sight for many of their friends who had only seen them as orthodox parents not given to displays of joy publicly.

The revelries lasted well into early Friday morning. The last of the guests left only around 3 a.m. Dipti, Ramnik and Parthiv were among those last guests to leave. Before leaving Parhiv told Bela, "I will pick you by 5 in the evening."

The Patels could barely catch a couple of hours of sleep. They got up by 6 and fixed themselves masala chai. Still joyous from their dancing the night before, the two decided to sit outside in their small backyard. It was a typical California morning. The sky was crisp and the air was invigorating. They sipped away for several moments before Dipti said, "Should we have advise him about protection?"

"You are really into this, aren't you, you naughty girl?" Ramnik said. It was after years that he had used the expression 'Naughty girl', which he used frequently in the flush of their young relationship.

Dipti felt shy but continued, "I think we should tell him to be careful. We don't want to be grandparents so early."

Ramnik laughed at her leap from using protection to becoming grandparents.

"Dipti, these days they know about all this much earlier. You should not be surprised if Bela carries it for him," he said.

"Do you think his time with Bela will change his mind?" Dipti said.

"Who can tell for sure but what I saw of him at Bear Valley tells me that he might have second thoughts but eventually he will go ahead. I think he sees this celibacy thing as a way of testing himself. It looks like a goal he has set for himself," Ramnik said.

"But then he should not even go with Bela and raise her hopes. I think it is being cruel. I hope the two of them have talked through this. I hope Bela recognizes that Parth may still leave her to join the Sansthan," Dipti said including several themes of her concerns.

"Well, they are both adults now. We may think of them as children but we have to step back. This is a very different time from when you and I were growing up. You remember I did not even hold your hands for months after we met?" Ramnik said.

"Let's not talk about our past. Let's talk about Parth's future. I am going to tell Ela to speak to Bela before they leave. Ela should tell Bela to do her best to compel Parth to change his mind," Dipti said.

Ramnik disapproved of the idea and said so. He thought that might be counterproductive. "Let this not become a plan hatched by us to dissuade him. He has to come to that decision on his own," Ramnik said.

By the time Ramnik left for his store at 10.30, Parth had not woken up. "Tell Parth to go via the store," Ramnik said and left.

Parthiv got up only around 1.30 in the afternoon. Dipti was catching a repeat telecast of her favorite soap "Teri Bindiya Mein Suraj Ki Lalima". The episode she missed last night because of the birthday party was crucial. All hell had broken lose because Suhani had caught Thakur peeping into her bedroom. She accused him of pursuing her out of lust.

When Parth came down, Suhani was vigorously pointing at Thakur and saying, "शमम िमर जाना चाहहए आपको जिन बहुको ऐी नज़र ि देखने के पहले। अब इिघर में या िी आप रहेंगे या मैं। यह फ़ै िला आज, इी िक़िहोगा।" The accompanying music was a combination of temple bells and drums.

Parth asked Dipti to explain what Suhani had just said. "Mom, why is she so pissed and that old dude so shocked?"

"Not now, Parth," Dipti said.

Parth fixed himself breakfast and started to go up to his room. Dipti called him back. "Wait, sit here with me. I want to talk to you. That woman is angry because she caught that man peeping into her bedroom."

"Why was he peeping into her bedroom? Isn't he too old for that?" Parth said.

"Lust does not go away. He has designs on her and she became wise to it. Now she wants him to get out of the house. Anyway, so tell me about your visit with Bela," Dipti said and realized that the segue from Thakur's lust to Parth's plan was terrible. She could not take it back.

"Mom, why are you talking about that old man's lust and my visit with Bela together?" Parth said in mock anger.

Dipti started laughing and said, "No son, it was a mistake but I could not do anything once I said it. But listen, both your father and I are very happy that you and Bela are together. There could be a future in that."

"Mom, it is just one weekend. Nothing has changed. I don't want you to think that anything has changed," Parth said.

"We will see after the weekend," Dipti said with a touch of mischief. "What is that supposed to mean?" Parth countered.

"You will find out yourself," Dipti said and started the soap episode she was watching on demand. "Whatever mom," Parth said and went up.

"Oh yeah, dad said you should drop by at the store before you go. So leave a bit early," Dipti said.

"Okay, I will leave at 4," he said.

Parth was at the store by 4.30. Ramnik was sitting in the lounge with Bela's father Mahendra. "Hey, dad. Hi Mr. Amin," Parth greeted the two.

"Mahendrabhai and I wanted to talk to you before you left. Both he and I are thrilled that you two are going to spend some time together. But remember that this comes with a lot of responsibility. Mahendrabhai knew about your wish to join the Sansthan but he thought it was one of those phases. I have told him that you seem serious. Given all that Mahendrabhai is not sure if it is a good idea for you and Bela to go for the weekend," Ramnik said.

Parthiv was surprised by the turn of events but did not say anything.

Mahendra took over from there. "Unless you have a long term plan with Bela I don't think you two should go on this trip. I have told her the same thing but she rejected my idea. She said she is 18 and grown up enough to take that decision. I cannot stop either one of you but as her father and your well-wisher I think you should reconsider one of the two things," he said.

Parth was at a loss for words. He finally said, "But you knew that I have plans to join Bear Valley. Bela knew too. This was entirely her idea. She told me on my 18th birthday that I should wait for her to turn 18 and the together we should decide after spending some time together."

"I agree and I am not here to stop you but to request you. She may have said that because she became emotional about it. Would you two at least talk it over before you leave?" Mahendra said in a tone full of entreaty.

Parth kept looking at the floor and then said, "Fine Mr. Amin. I will talk to her personally. I am going there now."

Although the idea of a celibate's life had consumed him for the better part of the last two years, he was equally looking forward to lovers' intimacies with someone he had known loved for so long. On his way to Bela's house, he thought about what he should do. Fortunately for him, Mahendra and Meena had already had a talk with Bela about the very subject. She was mentally prepared to hear it from Parth.

Bela was home alone. Her mother had deliberately left the house to give them some privacy. Much of Bela's radiance the night before was still in evidence except that she was now dressed in a shirt and jeans.

She jumped and hugged him hard. Before he could say anything, she started to kiss him. He found himself responding rather eagerly. It was their life's first passionately wet kiss. She grabbed his hand and led him to her room.

Parth asked, "But what about your mother?"

"Shut up and just come with me. No one's home," she said.

Bela shut the door behind her even as she unbuttoned herself. Parth sat on the bed looking at her in utter awe. He had never seen her like that. Her fabled body was barely covered in lingerie that she said had been gifted by her mother.

"Boy, you look like a supermodel," Parth said.

"Wait till you see this," Bela said and went inside her walk-in closet. She reappeared, jauntily swaying on her red high heels.

Parth was so overcome with desire that for the next one hour the Sansthan, Raghu Vishwa, Dhiru, and virtues of celibacy evaporated from his memory in the heat of their passionate lovemaking. Initially, both were awkward since it was the first time for each. However, soon their bodies had discovered their natural rhythm. It was as if they were living up to their years of being in love.

Parth and Bela called their fathers separately to inform that they had decided not to go to the Big Sur. Ramnik and Mahendra were relieved. Dipti was disappointed and Meena intrigued by the turn of events. None of them knew what was expected to happen in the Big Sur had already happened at home.

CHAPTER 18

Post-coital depression was not a term that Parthiv knew but without realizing, he felt a version of it the next morning at his home.

A dream where Guruji chastised him and caned him woke him at 4.30. The dream was quite vivid and the caning felt real. He did not remember any instance when he had woken up that early before. He sat up in his bed and thought about the evening with Bela. The image of her in her lingerie and heels and swaying was etched in his mind. The more he tried to banish the image, the more animated it became.

Between a stern Guruji and a desirable Bela, Parth felt terribly torn. He picked Guruji's book about celibacy from under his pillow and began reading it in the hope that it might help him deal with his conflict. He opened the most dog-eared chapter titled 'When Desire Comes Calling.' It particularly dealt with the "Temptations of Teenage".

"Desire for the female body is the most powerful force in a teenager's life. It is a blinding desire, which prevents you from seeing anything else. The world ceases to exist when you see a naked girl. It weakens you thoroughly. You lose your mind and are swept by the sheer force of *Kaam* (Lust). That is the best time to stop oneself and chant mantras. Chanting pacifies your *Kamuk* (lustful) and disobedient mind and tames it. Celibacy is a hard discipline but an essential discipline for teenagers accepting the life of a monk," one passage said.

Quite reflexively, Parth started reciting the Gayatri mantra even though it was never prescribed as an antidote to a teenager's raging hormones. It was probably autosuggestion that was working but the mantra seemed to settle down his mind in ferment. He kept repeating the mantra for the next 30 minutes. It helped him only marginally as the memory of Bela's body aroused him yet again. He started pacing in the room. It was by 6 a.m. that he got a text alert on his mobile. The tone told him it was from Bela who had texted him a picture of her in the lingerie with the words "Mmmm..." Before he could respond, one more picture came. This time it was a close-up of her cleavage. "Spectacular, aren't they?" The text said.

"Stop it, Bela. Not now. I am going through something," Parth texted back. She replied, "Are you fantasizing about me?"

"BELA, I SAID STOP IT," he said clearly showing his annoyance.

There was no response from her after that.

Ramnik and Dipti were already up and were in the kitchen, having their tea. They were unaware of Parth's state of mind. They thought he was still sleeping.

Dipti asked, "What do you think happened between those two?" Ramnik did not respond. He was reading the papers.

"Do you think anything happened?" she persisted. Ramnik still did not respond.

Finally, Dipti said, "I asked you something."

Barely looking up, Ramnik said, "How do I know what happened? It is not our business to know that now. They are both 18."

"You make 18 sound like some magical border where parents just vanish from their children's lives," Dipti said somewhat irritated.

"All that I am saying is that we have to wait for him to share if he wants to share," Ramnik said, "Now please don't ask him for details."

"If I want to ask, I would. I want to know whether our son is staying or going. I want to know it now," Dipti said.

By 8.30 Parth was on his mobile talking to Dhiru. He called him Kaka.

"Kaka, I am ready to join now," he said. There was a stunned silence at the other end.

"Have you thought this through? Because we need your parents' permission too," Dhiru said. "I am 18, Kaka. I need no permission," Parth said.

"In Indian culture you need parents' permission at any and all ages. Besides, the Sansthan has a policy of formal consent," Dhiru said.

"So I will tell mom and dad and you talk to them too. I want to start this week," Parthiv said with a determination that made Dhiru uncomfortable.

"There are procedures and rules that we must follow. It is not like you just drive up to Bear Valley and renounce the world. It is not that simple," Dhiru said.

"Kaka, it is that simple. I read Guruji did just that. I am ready to do it too," Parth said.

"I suggest you first talk to them and then let me know so that I can call them both," Dhiru said. Parthiv knew that Ramnik left for the store by 11 a.m. He went down right away.

The parents were still in the family room. Dipti was dusting while Ramnik was immersed in the newspapers. Dipti noticed him first.

"Uthi gayo? Kem chho?" Dipti asked him.

"Hi mom, hey dad. Yeah mom, uthi gayo," he said. "Want some breakfast?" Dipti asked.

"Not hungry yet," Parth said.

He went and sat across Ramnik while Dipti continued to dusting and arranging. Parth checked his mobile. No text yet from Bela after his curt response.

"Mom, dad, I have decided to go. I want to go this week," Parth said.

Dipti skipped a heartbeat hearing that but pretended she did not understand. "Go where? Are you to going the Big Sur?" she asked.

"No mom. I meant Bear Valley," Parth said.

That got Ramnik's attention as he folded the newspaper and asked, "What?"

"Dad, you heard me. I have decided to join the Sansthan and become a celibate monk," Parthiv said.

The Patels were frozen. Finally, Dipti regained her composure and asked, "Didn't you and Bela do anything?" As soon as she asked, she realized the ridiculousness and desperation of her question.

"What's wrong with you mom? I am not discussing that," Parth said sounding very annoyed.

"No son, we are discussing everything now," Ramnik said. "This has gone on long enough. Your mother is right to demand to know. We are your parents. You may be 18 but we are still your parents. This is not James' or George's house. Understand? We will demand to know."

Ramnik sounded angry and forceful. His eyes had widened and nostrils flared. Dipti had dropped the dusting cloth on the floor and stood with her hands akimbo.

"We need to resolve this now. I cannot live in this terrible uncertainty. What has gotten into your head, Parthiv?" Dipti said.

"I don't get this. All my life you both have gone on and on about Indian values and culture and religion and all that stuff. Guruji this and Swamiji that is all I have heard for years. Mom, you could not stand Bela wearing shorts and T-shirt and now you are desperate to ensure that I slept with her. Yes, we had sex. We loved it but I feel terribly guilty and I have decided to become a monk to redeem myself," Parth said in one breath.

Dipti started crying while Ramnik just sat there looking lost.

"I have already spoken to Dhirukaka this morning. I called him and told him. He insisted it was not that simple. There is a way to do it including your consent. I want your consent," Parth continued.

The Patels could not bring themselves to respond. For the first time after their marriage, Dipti saw Ramnik cry.

Parth, who was so far pressing on unmindful of his parents' feelings, noticed how bent his parents looked by this sudden onslaught. He too started to sob uncontrollably.

Ramnik got up and embraced him. "Dikra (son), we cannot stop you but we cannot consent either," he said.

Dipti had stopped crying. She looked stern but thoughtful. She said, "Let's get this over with. You have my blessings. Go ahead and become a monk. I will learn to live without you."

The emotional roller-coaster went on for some more time. After the initial shock had worn off, the Patels recognized the futility of standing in his way. They knew even if they prevented him, they would have to deal with an unhappy son every day. Parth was always stubborn and unyielding once he made up his mind.

Ramnik called Dhiru. The two talked at length about what it meant. They also talked about the regimen Parthiv will have to follow for the rest of his life. They discussed the consent form. Dhiru asked if they would like to wait and weigh their options. Ramnik and Dipti both said no on the speaker phone. Parth heard them patiently.

"So I am going to email you the consent form today. I will also speak to Swamiji. He will be very very pleased. Parth is coming to his second home," Dhiru said.

The call ended. The Patels looked at each other, smiled, hugged and cried again. "Mom, we can always meet. Can we not dad?" he said.

"Trust me son, your life will undergo a very major change. The Sansthan is a very demanding place. But you have made your choice," Ramnik said.

Parthiv went up to his room and called Bela.

She did not answer. He left a voicemail saying, "Hey Bells. Last evening was magical. You were like a dream. But I think that dream is not for me. I have decided to join the Sansthan. Call me. There may not be many more opportunities to call after this."

She did not.

CHAPTER 19

Leaving home felt to Parth what leaving his mother's womb must have felt like but he had no memory of that. He hoped that in good time he would forget the wrenching pain of leaving. After contemplating it for over a year and half, during which he had swung between love and lust, Parthiv was face to face with his departure.

He had sketchy sleep the night before with Bela dominating most of his dreams. Her swaying lingerie walk on high heels was a recurring image in those dreams. He was embarrassed to discover in the morning that he had had a wet dream during one of those walks. He took a long bath to cleanse himself of the guilt that followed.

To make the mood more melancholic, the sky was overcast and the clouds were a color confused between slate and sepia.

It had not started to rain but Dipti had not stopped crying all morning that Saturday. All these months, Parth's departure had seemed like a teenage itch that would subside. She believed that in time Bela's draw on her son would grow enough for him to forget about the Sansthan. She was wrong.

Parth came down wearing shorts and T-shirt. He betrayed no anxiety or worry. He greeted Dipti with the same effusive, "Hey mom" as he climbed down two steps at a time. In those 16 steps from the bedrooms down to the kitchen, which took a couple of seconds, Parth's entire life played out in front of Dipti. She did not say anything in return and merely kept looking at him as he came and hugged her hard. He would not let go of her for about a minute. She shook as she sobbed. Finally, she said in a quivering voice, "I have made everything that you love because this is the last time you will be eating your favorite food."

Parthiv had not thought about that. Strangely, of all things that should have made him feel the pain of leaving, it was the realization that he would not get his favorite food that caused him the most anguish. He had a tough time fighting the lump in his throat. He started crying as well. Ramnik came down and saw the mother and son looking distraught. He was overcome by emotions but he managed to retain his composure.

"You know son, you don't have to do this. It is true that we kept telling you about the virtues of the Sansthan and nobility of celibacy but we never really thought that you would join that. Now that you have grown up and you are here with us and we see you every day doing your things and then you will be gone soon......" Ramnik trailed off and broke down like Parth or Dipti had never seen him do. He was inconsolable for several minutes. Dipti seemed to have calmed down but it was more resignation than calm. She had a vacant look in her eyes.

Parth started to eat but he could not push the food down. The lump was still blocking the way. He started crying again. All three could feel the others' pain but none of them went close to each other to console. Their sorrow was common but their sharing was not.

In a measure of how the human mind fortifies itself quickly against tragedies and invents ways to console itself, Dipti was now imagining how the regimental life of a celibate monk, without the kind of freedom to seek pleasure at whim that Parth has become accustomed to, may eventually force him to return. Of course, there had been extremely few instances of monks having left the order or being allowed to leave the order. For a vast majority of the monks, the Sansthan was a strict one way street which led them in and had no way out other than revolt. Dipti was debating in her mind whether Parthiv too would come to a stage where he might feel compelled to rebel. For her to think of that even before he had been formally initiated was probably a trick that mother's mind was playing.

The Patels had planned to leave for Bear Valley at 2 p.m. Ramnik saw no point in waiting that long and instead suggested that they leave right away. It was only 10 a.m. Dipti was surprised to hear that but understood when Ramnik explained: "Two hours are not going to change his decision. They are not going to lessen our pain. So why wait?"

Although neither said as much, both knew well that at some level they felt a sense of pride that their son was joining the order of his own volition unlike many others, one immediate case in point being Jay. For years, the parents subtly and not so subtly conditioned Parth about the virtues of monkhood and when the time came, they were happy that it was his decision. The passage of nearly two years between the time he first decided to join and the day he was leaving meant that he had had enough opportunity to weigh his options, including the one to spend his life with Bela. In not choosing to do so, he may have done what his parents had once wished for but he was doing so as a choice and not an imposition.

The drive to Bear Valley was surprisingly free from tension or sadness. Somewhere along, all three had come to terms with the decision after a particularly emotional morning. On an impulse, Parth texted Bela: "Driving with dad and mom to Bear Valley. By this time tomorrow, I will be a monk." He got no response until they reached the Sansthan compound. That is when he got a reply: "Are you asking me to change your mind? You had your shot, dude." He knew she was angry. Just as he was about to call her, came another text, "Don't bother to call. I don't date monks."

Dhiru was waiting for the Patels in the "Receiving Hall". He greeted them with great warmth. Parth bent down to touch his feet. Dhiru blessed him with an odd sentiment, "May you prosper." He realized his mistake and laughed. "May you prosper spiritually," he corrected himself. He turned to Dipti and Ramnik to say, "We are so grateful. Swamiji is immensely pleased to have Parth among us. He sees something special in him. I know this is an emotional day for you but you will soon understand that this is best for him and us."

Dhiru explained that while the initiation into monkhood was scheduled only a week from that day on Guru Purnima, the Sansthan always insisted on a week of orientation to the life in the ashram. "It does take a lot of getting used to. Parents often do not realize the difference between being just visitors on special occasions and committing their sons to live here for the rest of their lives. This orientation is very necessary," he said.

Dipti and Ramnik thought the initiation was the very next day after the ritual tonsuring ceremony. "No, that's just the beginning. We don't say this publicly but as your friend I can share this with you. This seven-day period of transition allows the monks to reflect on their decision to join the order. We do not want those who are not ready to come in but are here under force or duress from their parents. You know we had that case in 2010 when this young man, Paresh, created so much controversy. We avoid that at any cost. Swamiji does not want anyone questioning our intentions," Dhiru said.

Dhiru was in the mood to talk some more but did not want to do it in the presence of Parth. Luckily for him, the monk in charge of orientation dropped by to say that Parth should come to the garbhagriha where the other four boys, including Jay, had already arrived. The atmosphere in the garbhagriha was more like an assembly of university freshmen. Jay looked crestfallen but cheered up when he saw Parth. They both hugged. "Fuck man, we are actually here, dude!" Jay said. A monk, who was going to give them initial orientation, heard Jay and said sternly, "Language, young man. You are no longer an ordinary person. You are going to be a monk. This is an ashram. We allow no profane language. Even dude ends here."

"Are you the drill sergeant?" Jay persisted even as the other four, including Parth, let out a whoosh of disbelief at his question.

The monk smiled and said, "You can call me that. My job is to make sure that you stay straight and narrow. Looks like we have someone really angry here."

Before Jay could say anything, Parth stopped him. "We are here. Let's be respectful. We came on our own," Parth said.

"No I didn't. My dad forced me to enlist. Like the marines, they will shave us off soon," Jay continued his tirade.

"Jay, you can still go back if you dislike it so much," Parth said.

"My parents just dropped me and left. They don't care what happens to me," Jay said. "You can go back with my parents tomorrow," Parth said.

"And you are staying?" Jay said.

"I came without any force. I intend staying," Parth said.

The six young men were asked to take a bath before they could be handed a white dhoti and a shoulder wraparound. The monk explained to them, "The white attire is only until you are tonsured tomorrow morning. After that, you will be given a set of two ochre dhotis and shirts. Those will be your permanent clothes. The ashram will give you a pair of shoes and slip-ons and other minimum personal effects such as a toothbrush, a bar of soap and two towels. Your stainless steel food plate, spoon and mug will be by your bedside. Your beds will be assigned tomorrow. You will be tonsured at 10 a.m. We allow only male family members to witness the tonsuring ceremony. Your actual initiation is still a week from today on Guru Purnima, the day when you celebrate your guru and pay your respect. There will be songs sung by our singing monk group in praise of Swamiji. There will be several lectures. The day will end with a havan, the lighting of the ritual fire, when the six of you will be initiated in an elaborate ceremony. I want you to know that the life here is happy but very demanding. You are all very young and full of desires and aspirations. All that will change once you become monks. We expect you to follow a strict routine starting at four in the morning."

Jay mumbled soft enough so that only Parth could hear. "I told you this is like a prison. You are being processed."

Parth agreed in his mind that the tone that the monk used was consciously unemotional and made to sound as if they were being prepared for some sort of punishment.

The monk continued: "This is an ashram with very strict rules of conduct. You are not here on picnic. You are here to uphold great Hindu traditions. You are here to learn. You are here as someone who has given up the worldly life. You are here in the service of the Sansthan and its glorious objectives. You may now go back to the Receiving Hall and be with your parents and family. We will call you again after sometime."

Jay and Parth went together. They were told that Parth's parents were in Dhiru's office. Jay looked particularly despondent. He told Parth to carry on because he wanted to sort out some things in his mind. "I am already losing it. Did you hear that asshole?" he said.

Parth did not say anything and went inside Dhiru's office.

"Here he is," Ramnik said as if he was meeting his son after a long gap. "How did it go?" Dipti asked.

"It was alright, mom. Tonight, we will be given white clothes after bath. We will be shaved tomorrow morning and then given orange clothes. There is a head shaving ceremony at 10 a.m. You can go after that. You can go now if you want," he said.

"No, I would like to be there when you are shaved," Dipti said. "But mom you know you won't be allowed in," Parth said.

"I know but I will be around. I want to see you as a monk in a monk's clothing," Dipti said and broke down.

The tonsuring ceremony was a quick affair, which only the young men's fathers were permitted to witness. For all his combativeness the previous day, Jay was strangely relenting. He said nothing as locks of his hair dropped on the floor. Parth sat calmly as his turn came. The monk shaving him gently pushed his head down and the clipper began whirring. That was the moment when Parth was overcome with profound doubt about what he was embarked on. Unlike Jay, who went in mocking and cursing but became reconciled, Parth's was the exact opposite response. He raised his head suddenly as if trying to stop the monk. His hair was entangled in the clipper that was still on. That caused considerable pain.

Ramnik, not expecting such a response from his son, said, "What's going on Parth?"

"Dad, I need a couple of minutes," he said and turned to the monk, "May I please have a couple of minutes. I will be right back."

The monk was intrigued but let him go with some reluctance.

Parth took his cell phone from his father and stepped out. He called Bela. To his surprise, she answered.

"Bells, don't disconnect. I need to talk to you," Parth said.

"If I didn't want to talk, why would I answer it? What's going on?" Bela said.

"They have just begun shaving my head. This is real. And I am not sure," Parth said. "So don't do it. Leave that place now," Bela said.

"No Bells, it is not that simple. I want to do it and I don't want to do it. It is like my first time with you that evening at your home," Parth said.

"Listen Thiv, we have gone through this many times. I am kind of fed up. I love you but can't help you if you don't want to be helped. I am here. Come back if you want to," Bela said and hung up.

Parthiv went back inside, sat down on the floor and waited for the monk to finish the job. His head shaved, he turned toward his father and then walked away to take bath. When he returned he was in a white dhoti, a white wraparound and flaming yellow smear on his forehead. He looked like a caricaturized version of himself. Ramnik was awestruck by his look. He had never seen him like that. He took a few pictures to show it to Dipti.

"Dad, I have to go now," Parth said and hugged Ramnik. He could feel his father's chest heaving. Jay, who stood next to them, was quiet and distant.

As the six men in all white walked away, Ramnik felt a gaping vacuum in his chest. He kept looking until they disappeared behind the door to the living quarters. He walked out of the hall. Dipti was waiting anxiously. He showed her the pictures on Parth's mobile phone. She smiled and cried. Then smiled some more and cried some more. After she handed the phone back to Ramnik, he said, "Parth wanted me to send these to Bela." He sent two. There was no response.

The Patels drove back in complete silence.

CHAPTER 20

Two days after the tonsuring ceremony, Jay began showing signs of ever darkening depression. With no mobile phone—a near organic extension of his gregarious personality—he looked utterly reduced in stature. Parth often caught him moving his thumbs in imaginary texting action. He was experiencing an unusual kind of withdrawal symptoms after losing his mobile phone.

The monk, whose task it was to ease the new recruits into the life of regimental renunciation, noticed the changes and brought it to Dhiru's attention.

"He looks pale and drawn. I am concerned about him. I think we should tell Swamiji and may be even his parents," the monk said.

Dhiru thought for a few moments and said, "Let's wait for a day or so. If he does not show any sign of improvement, I will tell Swamiji and his father."

On the third day of their stay in the ashram, Jay finally spoke to Parth. "I miss banging chicks, man. It is only the third day today and I feel weird in my pants errr dhoti. I don't know how I am going to do without it for the rest of my life," he said.

Parth noticed that while the language was very much trademark Jay, the tone was downbeat and defeated. He sounded unusually stripped of his naturally confrontational style.

"Are you depressed, Jay?" Parth asked.

Jay was surprised by the question but answered, "Yeah, I am depressed. Who lives without sex? Ever? And why?"

Parth laughed and said, "It's a good question. I have signed up for this life knowingly. I know you have not. You can still go back."

"Dad told me if I ever came back he would disown me. Where am I going to go after leaving here? I am fucked without getting laid," Jay said.

"If you are so affected by this, I can ask my dad to help you. You still have some days before the initiation. You can always get out. You can leave even after the initiation. The ashram cannot force you to stay," Parth said.

"You don't know my dad. He gets violent," Jay said and lifted his dhoti to show a deep blue mark on his right thigh. "Two days before coming here, we had an argument and he hit me here several times with a screw driver."

Parth was stunned at the revelation. He could not form a response immediately. He had no idea that Jay's father was a violent man given to beating his son. His reputation outside was very different. He stayed quiet for several moments as Jay welled up. He had never seen Jay cry. In a span of a few moments, his immediate world was rudely turned inside out.

He finally said, "Really? I mean are you serious, Jay? How can this be?"

Despite his orthodox views, Jasubhai was known to be jovial towards others. No one would have thought that he abused his son. Their differences were well known among the community but that was about all.

Jay kept looking down without saying a word. He looked lost and distant. This dramatic change of personality was making Parth very uncomfortable. He had half a mind to talk to Dhiru. He did not know that the monk in charge of their transition had already alerted Dhiru.

"Why didn't you ever tell me this? We all would have helped. This is abuse, Jay," Parth said.

"I know but I thought I would be able to deal with it myself. I thought wrong. Now I am here, stuck forever. I should kill myself," Jay said.

"What are you saying, Jay? I am going to Dhiru uncle right now," Parth said and got up to leave.

Jay grabbed his hand and said, "Don't. They are all part of the same racket. I do not want you to say anything to anyone. Promise me that."

Parth sat down and let out a sigh. "I have to do something. I am worried now," he said.

"You don't have to do anything. Just be with me when you can. I don't like this place. It looks pretty but is actually quite weird," Jay said.

Their conversation was interrupted by the monk who came to announce it was time for them for their orientation hour.

It was inside a small classroom with 30 benches. Only six of them were occupied by the new recruits. They all sat upfront.

The monk said, "Swami Hariratna will be here soon. He is a revered saint who prepares new monks for their life ahead. He has trained several hundred monks here in America, Canada and India. Pay attention to every detail he talks about. You may ask questions but only when he says you can."

"This is sucking big time," Jay whispered so that only Parth could hear.

Swami Hariratna was a tall man, perhaps unusually so for a monk. Like many tall men, he walked with a slight stoop as if to tell those shorter than him that he was not that different. At 6 feet 5 inches, it would always appear as if he gangled into any place rather than normally walk into it. He had a stern face, made even more so by his bushy black eyebrows that made him look as if he always doubted your intentions.

He quickly surveyed the young men and instinctively decided to train his gaze on Parth. He thought Parth had that attentiveness which was very important during such orientation. He did notice Jay's sullen face but chose to disregard it.

"Namaste. I am Hariratna which means 'God's gem'. I am not God's gem. It is just a name. Welcome to the Sansthan. Your life of worldly pleasures is about to end. Let no one tell you otherwise. Joy here is of a different kind, it is a joy of having no attachment. It is a very hard path full of obstacles but if you keep walking those will melt away. Here at the Sansthan, we expect you to commit yourselves 100 percent to our causes and His (he emphasized his to make sure they understood he meant God) plans. You are not here on a summer break. This is your life now.

Pleasures as you have understood so far will disappear. You are at an age where sex is always on your mind. Our mission is to help you sublimate it. Sex is a form of energy that you must divert to other pursuits. That is why celibacy of body as well as mind is important. You are not only giving up sex in your body but also in your mind. This is a primary condition to be a monk here. We do not think less of women. We simply do not think about them. There is a big difference between the two. You will understand it as you learn more. I have spent a lifetime learning that.

We allow no contact with women, including your mothers. It is a connection you must all sublimate. We expect you to keep Guruji's book 'Celibacy and Restraint: Ingredients of a Happy Life" with you as a guide and inspiration. Guruji said, "It falls only on the chosen ones to lead a life of celibacy and restraint. It is a tough path to follow but eventually the only worthwhile path to follow." You are about to embark on that path. By tonsuring, you have taken the first step on that path.

As the first exercise after your initiation, we would ask you to spend one full day thinking about your fantasies about women. That is the only way for you to push them out of your life. Sex is not wrong. It is just not for a monk. It is a great sacrifice since there is no monkhood without sacrifice. We will teach you ways to conquer your desires through scriptures and postures. We will ensure that you reach a stage of the ultimate sublimation of desires."

Hariratna's monologue went on for about 45 minutes in a near somnambulant tone. Parth, who had so far displayed great resolve to take to monkhood, was beginning to wonder whether it was a sensible thing to do. At the end of the monologue, Hariratna asked the young men, "You may now ask any questions."

"Can we masturbate?" Jay asked so instantly that Hariratna was a bit unsettled. "Masturbation is forbidden. It is like surrendering to your very base desires," Hariratna said. "How would you know if we did masturbate?" Jay persisted making Parth rather squeamish.

"We can tell but, more importantly, we expect you to honestly adhere to the rules of the order," Hariratna said, trying hard to contain his irritation.

"How can you tell? It's not like the color of my skin is going to change," Jay said.

The monk in charge of transition tried to intervene but Hariratna raised his hand and stopped him. "No, that's fine. Let him ask as many questions as he wants. He is a troubled child," Hariratna said.

Jay laughed and said, "This child is 21 and not troubled. You are troubled."

There was an audible gasp at Jay's insolence even among that small assembly.

Hariratna, still maintaining his composure, said, "We are all children and I am not ashamed to say that we are all troubled, some more so than the others."

"I am here because my dad forced me. I don't believe in any of this. I like girls, I love girls, and I enjoy every part of their body," Jay said.

By now Hariratna was at the end of his patience but being who he was he could not show it. The monk had slipped out and gone to Dhiru's office. Moments later Dhiru appeared, paid his respects to Hariratna and said, "Let me talk to Jay in my office."

Jay left with Dhiru.

With the flow of the meeting disrupted, Hariratna waited for a few moments to gather his thought and conclude the meeting. However, another recruit, Rakesh asked, "Swamiji, is being celibate the main goal of being here or there is something more?"

The question may have seemed polite in comparison with Jay's combative style but it was, in fact, as challenging.

"That is the kind of question we will reflect upon after the initiation. I am glad your minds are ticking. Hundreds of monks have gone through me over the years and these are all very natural questions. Asking a man in his late teens or early 20s to give up sex for life is indeed asking him for the moon. But we know how to do it. That should be all for today."

The recruits all touched Hariratna's feet one by one. After he exited the room, Parth continued sitting on his bench reflecting on what happened. Unlike Jay, who had no filters or brakes, Parth was able to take time processing information. Also unlike Jay, his reaction that followed was always very well considered and often dramatic. In a way, the nasty bullying at school had prepared him well not to react in a kneejerk fashion.

What he heard from Hariratna had already made him seriously rethink his decision to become a monk. However, he was nowhere close to the breaking point unlike Jay who began there. He wondered about what may have transpired between Jay and Dhiru but knew it could not be pleasant for either. Jay returned after 15 minutes looking chastened and shaken. He was shivering.

"What's wrong, Jay? What happened in there?" Parth said.

"I need to speak to my dad before I tell you. The bastard is sacrificing me for his sins," he said.

CHAPTER 21

The sins that Jay referred to dated back to 2010 when during one of his visits to Edison, New Jersey, Jasu had come into contact with Paresh Mehta's parents.

Sensing an opportunity to exploit his situation, Jasu had instigated Paresh's parents to go public with their son's complaints against the Sansthan. He had even suggested that the Mehtas should consider suing the Sansthan for damages on the grounds that they had kept Paresh under duress and by brainwashing him caused him serious mental anguish.

Although the Mehtas eventually decided against filing a lawsuit, it was at Jasu's instance that they told their story to *The Edison Examiner.* In the next couple of years, rumors started doing the rounds of the Sansthan community that it was Jasu who had manipulated the Mehtas into going public to use the pretext to extort money and favors from the Sansthan leadership. Some of the money thus extracted went as a loan to Ramnik, who had no idea about how the sum came about.

It turned out that the unauthorized television footage aired as part of the controversial documentary *"And the Ganga flows through America"* was not only supplied by Jasu but even shot by him unbeknownst to the Sansthan authorities. Jasu managed to play both sides for nearly three years after the 2010 Paresh Mehta affair. However, things began to unravel for him when the Sansthan leadership in general and Raghu Vishwa in particular eventually took an unyielding stand against his blackmail. They confronted him and said they would make his machinations known to the Sansthan followers. Fears of being publicly shamed and ostracized by his own community weakened his position to the extent that the Sansthan gained the upper hand. One consequence of that was that the Sansthan forced him to commit Jay to the order if he wanted it the disclosures about his involvement with Paresh Mehta and unauthorized footage quiet.

When Dhiru told Jay about all this, he was furious. He attempted to assault Dhiru but the monk in charge of transition restrained him. It took Dhiru several minutes to pacify him. Dhiru explained that it was Jasu's malicious conduct that had started it all. He also said he sympathized with Jay but could do nothing about it.

When Jay came out of Dhiru's office looking chastened and shaken, these disclosures were weighing him down. He was thoroughly confused and enraged. He became angrier when he was not allowed to call his father directly. He suggested to Parth that the two sneak into Dhiru's office to make a couple of phone calls. They found the opportunity the next day when Dhiru had to leave the campus for some official business. The main administrative wing of the ashram was a quiet place with hardly any staffers. Dhiru had his personal office apart from Raghu Vishwa who rarely came in. There was a small secretarial room adjacent to Dhiru's office where a secretary-cum-office manager worked five days a week. Mondays and Tuesdays were off for him.

Since Jay and Parth had not yet been initiated, they enjoyed a relatively unfettered stay at the ashram unlike other ordained monks who could not stray an inch from their routine and territory without being intercepted and punished.

That Tuesday morning Jay and Parth went into Dhiru's office to make their calls. The first of those was from Jay to his father Jasu. Jasu was shocked to receive the phone call. He knew about the ashram rules that strictly prohibited monks and others from making phone calls without direct authorization from Dhiru. It so happened that Dhiru had gone to meet Jasu to discuss a potential problem arising out of Jay's conduct and the two were together when Jay called.

"Dad, I want you to say nothing. Today I talk and you keep your mouth shut. You can't hit me on the phone. You screwed me because you are a criminal. You sold me to the ashram and did not even make any money. I will avenge this, dad. Dhiru uncle told me everything, about how you blackmailed the Sansthan and extorted money and then sacrificed me to buy your peace. You suck. You are disgusting, dad," Jay said in one breath.

Parth, who was used to Jay's ways, was still appalled at what heard.

All that Jasu could do is to ask, "How did you manage to get inside Dhirubhai's office?"

Before Jay could answer, Dhiru came on the line and said, "Leave my office right now. I am going to call Swami Hariratna on his mobile right now. If you resist, I will authorize him to call the police."

"Yeah. Go ahead and call the police. I will tell them you have kidnapped me and you are keeping me here forcibly," Jay said.

Dhiru and Jasu did not expect that move from Jay. Thinking quickly, Dhiru changed his tone and said, "I am sorry I did not mean that. I am returning this evening. Let us talk. I promise to tell you more about you but you have to promise not do anything crazy until I come back."

Jay thought for a while, consulted Parth and said, "Alright, I will wait until you return."

Dhiru passed the phone back to Jasu but Jay cut it off saying, "There is nothing to talk to you about."

As Parth and Jay waited, they spoke about many things, particularly how Jay never felt loved by his father. It was always an adversarial relationship ever since he became an adult but even when he was younger, Jasu treated him with an aloofness that Jay did not really understand. A lot of his rebellious behavior was a way to gain Jasu's attention, which was never the kind that he desired. The beating with the screwdriver was apparently not an uncommon feature in the way Jasu established his paternal authority. In the past, the screwdriver was replaced by whatever domestic object was available.

Parth could not come to terms with the fact that through all that abuse not only did Jay not call the police but even share anything with him or other friends. Suddenly, a lot of Jay's frequent odd behavior made sense to Parth now. It was someone who had endured a great deal of abuse.

The two were about to find out that there was much more.

Dhiru returned by 6.15 p.m. and went straight to Raghu Vishwa's room. He knew Jay was waiting for him but it was more important that he first shared with Swamiji what he had found out from Jasu. It was deeply disturbing but not out of character.

Swamiji finished his walk by 6.30 and returned to his room. He was expecting Dhiru because Dhiru had alerted him about wanting to discuss an urgent matter personally.

The two men had known each other for so long they almost never exchanged pleasantries or engaged in small talk.

"We potentially have a problem with Jay," Dhiru said.

Raghu Vishwa finished drinking water but did not say anything. He expected Dhiru to continue and finish describing the nature of the problem.

"Jasubhai told me that Jayendra was adopted as a child and has never been told about it," Dhiru said.

It was not for nothing that Raghu Vishwa had a reputation for being unruffled in the face of grave crises. As problems go, this one was not that minor but was not a crisis for the Sansthan either.

"In fact, Jasubhai admitted that the main reason why his relationship with his son has become more apathetic is because he is not his natural offspring. I also found out something more disturbing. It seems Jasubhai has beaten Jayendra all his life, the last being just two days before he came here," Dhiru said. For good measure, he described in some detail how Jasu had used a screwdriver.

Although Dhiru was accustomed to Raghu Vishwa's equanimity, he was surprised that the news of such abuse did not prompt any outrage from him.

Raghu Vishwa was quiet and immersed in deep thought. Dhiru knew that there was a lot churning behind that calm visage. Raghu Vishwa finally spoke, "I have known about all this for years."

Dhiru, who was standing all this time, crashed into a chair out of complete shock.

"I did not say anything because so far it was their domestic problem and I had no business getting involved. Now that Jayendra is here with us, it is our business as well. The first thing we must ensure is that we shield Jayendra from this. Let us not say anything to him, for now at least. Let us not get into a battle with Jasubhai either. As for Jayendra's conduct, leave that to me. I will deal with him. That is all there is to it," Raghu Vishwa said.

He spoke the last sentence with a firmness that Dhiru knew meant there was absolutely no room for any more discussion on the subject.

"You have had a long day. You should retire. Please have your dinner first. Dharemdrabhai (the cook) has outdone himself with kadhi and rice," Raghu Vishwa said in a somewhat labored effort to cushion the blow of what he had just let Dhiru in on.

Dhiru said yes with a forced smile and left. He went to his office to meet Jay. He was not happy to see that Parth was also there.

"Parth, I need to speak to Jayendra alone," Dhiru said.

"No Dhiru uncle, Parth stays. He must know what I know," Jay insisted.

"Actually, there is nothing much to say for now. I just met Swamiji. He is going to talk to you tomorrow. He has promised to settle all your doubts and fears," Dhiru said, sounding unconvincing.

He escorted Jay and Parth out and closed the office.

"I am hungry. I am told the kadhi and rice are delicious tonight. You two should eat as well," Dhiru said and abruptly left.

CHAPTER 22

The night for both Jayendra and Parth was spent convulsing in unpleasant dreams.

Jayendra could sense that there was something very important that had been held from him by Dhiru but he could not quite put a finger on it. Parth could sense that his mind had changed dramatically about his decision to join the Sansthan but was not quite sure what was causing the shift. Hariratna's harangue about celibacy was certainly one major part of that.

Jayendra was called to Raghu Vishwa's office at 9 a.m. Before leaving, he told Parth, "Wish me luck. I have a bad feeling about this." Parth hugged him.

Raghu Vishwa's office was a minimalist setting. He had a two feet by four feet oak wood desk and an old rosewood chair, the latter a legacy of Guruji. There was a vase in the right hand corner with fresh flowers from the ashram's garden, including anise. In the center was a much used copy of the Bhagvada Gita. He sat erect and appeared to be in deep meditation. Jayendra stood in the doorway for a few seconds.

"Come in, come in Jayendra. How are you?" Raghu Vishwa greeted him. "I am not too well, Swamiji. I have questions," Jay said.

"We all do, son, we all do. That's why you are here where you can find some answers," Raghu Vishwa said. "I have to tell you something but before I do, I want you to promise me that you will stay calm."

Jayendra looked intrigued and said, "I cannot make any promise. I am not a monk yet. I feel what I feel and I say what I feel."

Raghu Vishwa looked at him closely, probably wondering whether it was wise to do what he was about to do.

"There is something your parents have not told you for a long time. Now that you are about to begin a new life here under our care, I think you should know. You were adopted as a child," Raghu Vishwa said and let the revelation sink.

Jayendra did not quite catch it at first because his mind had wandered off. "What's that?" he asked. "You were adopted as a child," Raghu Vishwa repeated in an even tone.

Jayendra seemed to shrink in his chair. He then straightened up. "What, why?" he said.

Raghu Vishwa realized that the revelation was affecting Jayendra at a level where he could not quite reach and process. He got up and went to Jayendra's side of the desk. He put his hand behind Jayendra's head and said, "You were adopted by Jasubhai and Jyotiben when you were an infant."

As the knowledge began to sink in, Jayendra suddenly rose. He was about to leave the room but Raghu Vishwa said, "You will hear me out. You have to."

"You were adopted after your natural parents were killed in an accident in India. You came to America as an infant with your foster parents who never disclosed even to the immigration that you were adopted," Raghu Vishwa said.

Jayendra sat down again, still unable to wrap his head around the full import of what he was being told.

"Why wasn't I ever told all this? When did you find out? Is that why my father hates me? Is that why he has packed me off here? Did he ever love me?" Jayendra finally managed to string many questions together.

"Jayendra, those questions do not matter now. You are here, with us. We will look after you," Raghu Vishwa said trying to sound as matter of fact as he could.

"No Swamiji, no. No, you hear me, that's no. I don't want to take this shit," Jayendra said unmindful of his language in Raghu Vishwa's presence. "I want to leave right now and talk to Jasu and Jyoti. Right now," he said and started walking towards the door. Before he could open it, it opened and Dhiru came in. He was waiting outside and heard the commotion.

Jayendra pushed Dhiru aside saying, "Dhiru uncle you lied to me." Dhiru tried to grab him but Jayendra was too strong and angry for him. He ran through the hall and stormed out of the main entrance. He was shouting, "I need a car. I need to call. Right now."

Hariratna, who happened to be on his way to the routine morning meeting with Raghu Vishwa and Dhiru, saw Jayendra. His imposing frame had a salutary effect on Jayendra as he stepped back and raised his hands to cover his face as if he was about to be slapped. It was a reflex action that he carried with him from home.

"What's going on? Why are you out here? Who authorized you?" Hariratna unaware of what had transpired said.

By now, Dhiru was already out. "Listen Jayendra, I am as angry as you are but anger will not solve this. I found out only yesterday. You want to go home, I will take you but come inside for now. We cannot make a scene," he said.

Jayendra had begun to calm down. Anger had given way to crying. He hugged Dhiru and sobbed.

After a couple of minutes, he said, "Dhiru uncle, I want to go back to Parth. I am going to tell him everything."

Parth was going through his own little upheaval. Hariratna's monologue about celibacy had affected him much more than he realized the previous day. There was a difference between reading Guruji's book and actually being inside an ashram and living the life of a celibate monk. He had been told by some of the new monks that many of their senior teachers happily violated

Guruji's tenets. A young monk, who had been ordained a year earlier, had told him that there had been instances of pornographic material being smuggled into the ashram.

To compound his problem, he could not get Bela out of his mind. Every time he thought of their time together, he felt unmanageably aroused. It was one thing to talk about voluntarily resisting physical attraction at home but quite another to be part of an ashram that actively and assertively repressed such desires. "You are not only giving up sex in your body but also in your mind" was one thought that he remembered from Hariratna's monologue the most. He was now more convinced than ever before that it was not possible to achieve that state.

He wrote in his diary that morning after Jayendra was called to Raghu Vishwa's office, "Thoughts about Bells never leave me. The image of her in the red lingerie and heels is always around. Now that I don't have her, I want her more. How am I going to spend my life like this?"

He was desperate to talk to Bela and discuss his desires. With no access to phone, he felt utterly stifled. He had taken Hariratna's advice to think about his fantasies about women, Bela in particular, rather seriously. That was all he could think about. At home, he never thought it would be so hard to practice celibacy. "You are not only giving up sex in your body but also in your mind" kept ringing in his mind. The churning reached a stage where he ended up saying aloud, "You cannot give up sex in body and mind." The other four boys, who were also in the room, were startled by his outburst.

Fortunately for Parth, at that very moment Jayendra returned. They all noticed his bloodshot red eyes and defeated demeanor.

"What's wrong, Jay? What happened?" Parth asked.

The two went out of the room and spoke for an hour before they were called for Hariratna's teaching. Parth was shaken to his core. His own growing doubts coupled with Jayendra's tragic story had unhinged them both. They had no choice but to go for the teaching.

The subject was "Sadhu Dharma" or a monk's code of conduct. "A true monk has no wants and no needs," Hariratna began and at once lost Jayendra's and Parth's attention.

That night, Parth and Jayendra had decided that the day of their initiation would, in fact, be the day of their liberation.

CHAPTER 23

Ramnik arrived early on the morning of Guru Purnima, the day of the initiation. The fathers of the other four were also there. Missing conspicuously was Jasu.

The six young men were now out of bounds for their fathers. Their heads were shaved again that morning and their clothes changed from white to saffron yellow. For the ceremony, they had to wear only their saffron yellow dhoti and an angavastram. No footwear was permitted before the ceremony.

A shiny brass and copper havan kund was installed in the center of the garbhagriha stage. There was a stack of sandalwood logs. On left were six red bajoths and on the right was a higher, more ornate platform. On the platform was kept a large red cushion. There was an assortment of samagri, ghee, six coconuts and incense sticks.

At precisely 7.32 a.m. the six young men were brought and made to sit on the bajoths. Hariratna accompanied them. They were followed by 350 monks, each one of whom carried their own orange mats. They all settled down in precisely aligned 10 rows of 35 each. The fathers of the new men were seated right in the front. Each one of them carried an envelope of $10,001.

There were half a dozen high-definition cameras, both mounted and handheld being operated by a crew of ten. They were not monks but volunteers who always shot the Sansthan videos. The event was being webcast live. There was an estimated audience of close to 10 million devotees in America, India and other parts of the world who were expected to watch the ceremony. Dipti, Jyoti, Ela, Meena, Mahendra and Bela had got together to watch the initiation ceremony at the Amins'. Dipti had also invited George and James. They were there as well.

When the camera spanned on the six and particularly on Jayendra and Parthiv there was a gasp among their family and friends sitting in Silicon Valley. Dipti and Jyoti became emotional while Bela looked away. "Look at Pee Pee. He looks cool," James said causing the rest to laugh. When Bela finally managed to look at Parth, she found him to be irresistible. It was perhaps the forbidden aspect of his impending life that attracted her even more. She was embarrassed in her private mind at all the lustful thoughts she had about him right then. As if on cue, Parth looked right into one of the cameras. He seemed to be looking at her directly.

When Raghu Vishwa came onto the stage, the assembly of monks rose to their feet and then prostrated to the chanting of "Guru Bhrama Guru Vishnu". Petals of marigold were hurled in the air by Dhiru and three other monks. The stage managers of the ashram had ensured that the lighting was perfect in its gentle rust yellow hues, creating an illusion of early morning sunlight inside the cavernous hall. Live sweeping shots of the sun rising over Bear Valley were interspersed with the shots inside and to the accompaniment of a recorded of "Guru Bhrama" set to Raag Hamsadhwani. The platform on which Raghu Vishwa was to sit was brilliantly lit to ensure that his projection on this important day for the Sansthan was pitch-perfect. The optics on such occasions was very crucial for the Sansthan's growth because Raghu Vishwa had long understood that people remember what they see and not always what they hear. What they were seeing that morning was a spectacle suffused in tones that lent an aura of regeneration. Even those who did not believe in the Sansthan's ideals or did not believe in religion were moved by the sheer aesthetics of the event.

After the recitation of several shlokas extolling the nobility of the guru, fire was put to the sandalwood logs as Hariratna poured ghee. The fragrance of the sandalwood was instant and soothing. The monks on the floor sat erect and in rapt attention as Raghu Vishwa started his address.

"Priya Sadhugan, Namaskar on this sacred day. I never fail to feel overwhelmed on this day by your generous affections for me and my utter devotion to Guruji. We live in mutual love and respect," he said. There was a wave of applause.

"Siddhi Prapti Sansthan has a long and glorious history of selfless spiritual service to all those who seek it. We do not ask for much in return. But we are mindful that we can survive and flourish only if persuade young men to join us from time to time. No institution can survive and thrive without people fully committed to it. This glorious morning I want to thank the parents of these six young men on stage who will soon be initiated into the life of high monkhood. It is never easy to let go of one who came into this world because of you. Now they are in our care. I promise you we will treat them as our children.

I commend these young men for choosing this life over a life they might have imagined for themselves. They will discover that the life of a monk, while always fulfilling, is never easy. It demands a lot because it returns a lot. I have been a monk since I was a boy and I know what the challenges are for a young boy to give up pleasures even before fully discovering them. Pleasures as you have understood so far will disappear. New pleasures, more selfless pleasures, will come into your life. So embrace them as we embrace you," Raghu Vishwa said and concluded. There was a thunderous applause not just in the hall but across the world where millions were watching.

However, the atmosphere at the Amins' was subdued and somber. Both George and James were briefly swept away by the show and Raghu Vishwa's words but they were brought back to reality when they heard him say "Pleasures as you have understood so far will disappear."

Parth also noticed that line which was used by Hariratna as well. It seemed like one of the Sansthan's talking points.

The initiation was not a very elaborate ritual but it was intense despite its briefness. The six were made to make several offerings of samagri and ghee and also recite a dozen or so shlokas and resolves. They were also made to take a series of oaths culminating into one final oath about celibacy. That is when Parthiv snapped. Rebellion had been building up in his mind since the previous day, first because he could not get Bela out of his mind and then because of what Jayendra had told him. Even before he finished the oath of celibacy, he rose. He surveyed the audience and then pulled the angavastram from around his neck. He held it aloft for a few seconds, walking around like a prize fighter with his championship belt. And then, he rudely threw into the flames of the havan kund. The flames leapt.

It was so unexpected that Raghu Vishwa, Dhiru and Hariratna simply froze. The monks on the floor were stunned. The live audience throughout the world was horrified and the gathering at the Amins' stupefied. Ramnik could not process the turn of events as he kept raising his hands in bewilderment.

Parthiv grabbed the microphone and started to rant. It was the sort of raging soliloquy that he did not think he was capable of. Something deep inside had broken and made him indescribably bold. It was an inspired performance where the mouth was his but the words seemed to be rising from elsewhere.

"I have reached the limits of my patience today. I have risen to end this farce. We must stop this crazy hypocrisy. For nearly a week, we have been repeatedly told about things that make no sense. We have been told to be truthful when very often the foundation here is based on complete lies. We have been told that we are here to advance our great cultural values when, in fact, what we are doing is repress young men many of whom have been forcibly brought and kept here. We have been told about equality between the sexes but women are not allowed anywhere inside this ashram. We have been told about the virtues of celibacy when many monks here smuggle in pornographic material. This is a fraud we have allowed to go on for too long. Well, no more. Bela, Bells to me, if you are watching this I am coming back. I am coming back even if you don't want me. Mom, I am coming back and I know you want me. Dad, you are here, I am sorry to do this but I want to come back home and I am coming back home," Parth said.

Parthiv's words were spellbinding for the monks in the audience, in particular the other five novitiates. They were so unexpected and so indicting that there were several moments of stunned silence. What happened then was even more startling for the Sansthan leadership. Each of the five novitiates rose and approached the copper havan kund. They all took off their angavastrams and threw them into the fire. A small puff of black smoke emanated from the havan kund prompting Hariratna to mumble under his breath "Ashubh…ashubh" (Inauspicious..inauspicious)." Moments later, the six novitiates walked off the stage led by Parth.

Raghu Vishwa and others realized the damage had already been done to the Sansthan's reputation by this completely unpredictable turn of events. They could have ended it at any time but they were so captivated by the sheer unpredictability that by the time they got wise to it, it was too late. This was unprecedented in the Sansthan's history except for the Paresh Mehta affair, which was handled with remarkable swiftness by Raghu Vishwa. In contrast, this was a live webcast, unedited and extempore. To compound it, Parthiv's outburst was so effective and the response to it from other five equally damning.

At the Amins', James and George started applauding even as Bela joined in after initial hesitation. Dipti could not contain her joy. Ela, Meena, Jyoti and Mahendra were hugging each other. Inside the hall, Ramnik finally came to terms with his son's conduct. Jayendra lifted Parth and started swirling around. Finally, Dhiru regained composure and took charge of the microphone and quickly announced, "We are deeply embarrassed by what we just saw. We promise a thorough investigation and also assure you that the Sansthan's reputation will not be allowed to be trifled with." The live webcast was stopped.

Raghu Vishwa stormed out of the hall, followed by Hariratna. The assembly was dismissed. Ramnik, who understood the gravity of the situation, grabbed Parthiv and Jayendra, and led them to the car. Just as they were leaving, Dhiru came running after them. He stood in the way and stopped the car. He asked Ramnik to come out. Ramnik came out with great trepidation. Dhiru went close to him and whispered in his ear, "This is exactly what the Sansthan needed. Please leave right now."

On the way back, Jayendra borrowed Ramnik's phone and called Jasu.

"Hey Jasu, I know everything. I am coming back to pick up my stuff and then leave for good, you dick," Jayendra said.

Ramnik, already reeling under the impact of Parth's rebellion, was too shell-shocked to react to the way Jay had spoken to his father. He did not fail to notice that Jay did not call him dad but "Hey Jasu."

EPILOGUE:

Parth's rant went to become a YouTube sensation notching up millions of views. For a brief while, he became a much sought after guest on television in America and around the world. He and Bela decided to rebuild their relationship slowly. Jayendra moved into his own apartment with Ramnik's help. Jasu and Jyoti separated. Jasu went back to India and Jyoti moved in with Jayendra after much discussion. Ramnik and Dipti were joyous to have their son back.

The Sansthan survived the blow with the help of a virtuoso public relations performance by Raghu Vishwa through a carefully orchestrated video statement. In that, among other things, he said, "I am grateful to Parthiv Patel for pulling us back from the precipice. It is an ideal lesson for all institutions like the Sansthan which have a larger good at heart but often end up taking a narrow path to it."

POETRY BOOKS BY BHARAT THAKKAR, PH.D.

Collections of English poetry

Humming Horizons (1995)
Magodi Mystic (2015)
Let me be Me (2017)
Nanoseconds of Nostalgia (2018)

Novel

Unsuitable Celibate (2018)

Collections of Gujarati poetry

Soneri Maun (1963)
Krupa Sparsh (1967)
Smruti na Zaran (1985)
Gunjati Kshitijo (1997)
Sarvale Chicago (2018)

BHARAT THAKKAR EDITED BOOKS
(EDITOR)

- Future of Leadership, Edited Nine Chapters, April 2018, ISBN 978-3-319-73869-7. Palgrave-McMillan Publishers, August 2019,

- Paradigm Shift in Management Philosophy, Edited Ten Chapters, Book published by Palgrave-McMillan Publishers, August 2019, ISBN 978-3-030-29709-1.

- Culture in Global Businesses, Edited Ten Chapters, Book published by Palgrave-McMillan Publishers, January 2021, ISBN 978-3- 030-60295-6.

- Standoff: Virus and Us, Edited Ten Chapters, Book Published by Xlibris, May 2022, ISBN 978-1-6698-1075-9

REMINISCING
BY MAYANK CHHAYA

Prof. Bharat Thakkar's literary pursuits, both in his native language, Gujarati and language of work, English are ceaseless. For someone who has been writing poetry and prose for some six decades, Dr. Thakkar is now, what I partly call-in jest, on autopilot. He takes off, cruises and lands as a reflex action.

In my having known him for over a quarter century, I have never known him not writing in either or both the languages. It is a passionate affair.

--Mayank Chhaya
Journalist & writer, Naperville, IL.

CPSIA information can be obtained
at www.ICGtesting.com
Printed in the USA
LVHW101226090223
738979LV00019B/451